To Kathy ~

I hope you enjoy
this story ~ It's Lots
of Fun!

As Long As I Have Lips

by
Jon D'Amore

Advice & Legal Stuff

As Long As I Have Lips ISBN: 978-0-9853000-7-4

Jon D'Amore and his writings are represented by Howard Frumes of the law firm Alexander, Lawrence, Frumes & Labowitz LLP.

Cover design and graphics by JT Lindroos – www.oivas.com

Print layout and and ebook formatting by Steven W. Booth, Genius Book Services – www.GeniusBookServices.com

Back cover photo by Gerald Van Kollenburg – www.gvank.com

Published by JMD
Printed in the USA
As Long As I Have Lips – First Edition

Table Of Contents

Acknowledgements

To repeat myself from my last book, one of the reasons I continue to write my stories is because people around the globe have told me I succeeded in my goal…which has always been to bring pleasure, entertainment and a smile to the world. As far as that other codicil mentioned on the Acknowledgements pages of THE BOSS *ALWAYS* SITS IN THE BACK, DEADFELLAS and THE DELIVERY MAN about wanting a comfortable, relaxing life for myself…let's just say I can't bitch. I mean, I still *can*. But why here, and why now? I prefer to continue to take these narratives within me and bring them to life. The fact that people continue to enjoy what I do is a rush not many can fathom.

Thank you all.

The happiness in my life has always been due to my parents, Ann and Carmine *'Rocky'* D'Amore. I love them and they will always be in my heart.

Thanks to: ~~Melicent D'Amore (again) for everything~~ Stuart Aion; Jennifer Duke Anstey; Glorie Austern; Kathi Barry; Steven Booth; Cameron Burke; Elizabeth Carbone; Michael D'Amore; Tom & Doris DeFranco; Peter Flora, Gail *'GB'* Geoia; George & Eileen Herberger; Ray Koonce; JT Lindroos; Diane Lombardi-Fleming;

Stan Morrill; Jeremy Oliver; Julia Peterson; Les Reasonover; Louise Rittberg; Eileen Saunders; Tom Sullivan; Lisa Tracy; Gerald Van Kollenburg; Ed Wright…all believers in the dream, and caring friends and relatives for life.

The remaining space on this page is for "industry people" who deserve some ink: The Writers Group of Studio City and The Screenwriters & Actors of Santa Fe, for giving me the creative support to believe in myself and my writing, and for inspiring me to bring each and every high point of my creativity to an even higher level. And most importantly and sincerely, Howard Frumes, my legal representative and a dedicated believer who stood at my side knowing it would finally happen. He's truly one of the good ones. Trust me on that.

Dedication

Carmine '*Rocky*' D'Amore & Ann D'Amore

December 20, 1925 & January 18, 1925

to

January 30, 1994 & December 10, 2019

"*Treat everyone with respect upon meeting them…then let them prove
if they're worth it.
If they prove they're not…say it to their face, then walk away from
them and their lives.*"

John Lennon

October 9, 1940

to

December 8, 1980

"*When you say she's looking good, she acts as if it's understood.
She's cool, ooh, ooh, ooh…girl, girl.*"

Foreword
by
Steven W. Booth

Jon D'Amore and I met because of books.

I was looking for someone to help me in my author services company back in 2011, and Jon was looking for some side work. At that time, he was thinking of publishing his memoir, *The Boss Always Sits In The Back*. As a favor—and to thank him for his excellent work on the e-books I needed to format—I offered to layout *The Boss*. Jon worked with me to get it just the way he wanted it.

Now let me be clear, Jon is a man who knows what he wants. He had me do some formatting that I would consider "unorthodox," but it got the look he wanted. My favorite change was his 3-hyphen dashes. He and I went round-and-round on the 3-hyphen dashes (because, naturally, m-dashes are better, right Jon?). That may seem technical, but that's the level of control Jon needed in order to get the look he wanted.

Jon and I have been friends since then. I've worked with him on each of his books (and actually read them!). Jon not only knows what he wants in a book, he knows how to deliver it. His writing is tight, it's compelling, and when he wants to be, he's really funny. He is one of the most disciplined writers I know, delivering great stories in record time. As an author myself, I can attest that writing novels (at least for me, but really for every *other* author I know except Jon) is a slog. Each of the eight novels I've written and published took two or three times longer than Jon took to write *As Long As I Have Lips* (which, I understand, was about five months). I'm also a publisher, and I see manuscripts that are in all sorts of states of readiness for publication, and Jon's are as fun and clean as they come. If I could afford to pay him what he's worth, I would make him an offer in a heartbeat…and certainly one he couldn't refuse.

If there's one word I would use to describe Jon, it's "sincere," and that sincerity comes through in his storytelling. Don't let his New Jersey tough-guy persona fool you. He's a hopeless romantic and a fiercely loyal friend. If there's one person I can count on to look out for me, it's Jon. And his understanding of how people think and operate permeates his stories. *The Boss* delves deep into the culture of loyalty and respect in the New Jersey Mob (Jon is what I call "mob-adjacent," though he will vehemently deny that the mob even exists if you ask him). *Deadfellas* overlays that culture with a generous dose of zombie goodness (six of my eight novels are zombie novels, and while Jon and I don't see eye-to-eye on zombie fiction, I can't argue with his creative use of the genre). *The Delivery Man* is possibly the most romantic hit-man novel I've ever read. And while no one dies in *As Long As I Have Lips,* Jon uses his understanding of how people think, act, and react to a sales pitch, whether it's an advertising campaign or the rituals of courtship. I won't go too deep into the story of *As Long As I Have Lips*—instead, I'll let you discover it on your own.

I am a big fan of Jon's stories, and I am a big fan of Jon. I think you will be too (now let's see if my m-dashes survive the formatting process!).

—Steven W. Booth
Los Angeles, California
February, 2020

Preface

What?

No Mafia? No zombies? No Mafia-zombies? No vigilantes or honest attorneys showing up at someone's door to blow their brains out? *What happened?*

Well, folks…what can I tell you?

It's just another slice in the evolution of my writing process. Many authors find their primary genre and stick with it…but I didn't want to be labeled as a "Mob writer" simply because my first book, The Boss *Always* Sits In The Back, was a memoir of my family, the guys involved in that lifestyle, the region of New Jersey where we lived from the 1950s to the late-1990s…and its proximity to New York City.

A *lot* of people asked, "When will you write a follow-up to The Boss?" Some even *demanded* one. But how? The majority of those I wrote about were either still incarcerated or dead due to natural causes or a sudden increase of lead in their bloodstream and organs. Plus…they had never done anything as fantastic as the Las Vegas scam they pulled off in the mid-to-late 1970s.

Having a slew of true stories that went unused in The Boss, and after the readers continually asked (or insisted) for another book, I took the horror-comedy screenplay Steve Barr and I co-wrote several years earlier and combined it with those actual unexploited accounts…resulting in the release of Deadfellas to satisfy those wanting another book. How was I to know it would introduce me to another group of followers? Who knew there were that many "Mob-Zombie" fans?

A year later I released the murder mystery, The Delivery Man. This was *also* based on true events, though I made sure each account resulted in a more adequate ending for the innocent *and* evil victims than what actually took place thanks to the legal system.

And again…readers around the world loved it. So who was I to bitch?

I always wanted to write a story based on a conversation I once had with a friend I've known since college…in addition to my wanting to write about older women and the younger men in their lives.

While living in New Jersey in the late-1980s, my friend asked me to join her at a Depression glass auction in Allendale. Having no idea what Depression glass was, she educated me during the drive. Once in the parking lot, we were, as usual, delayed in getting out of my car because she needed to lower the sun-visor, open the mirror, turn on the light and apply a coat of her ever-present lipstick.

Having been friends as long as we had, and after witnessing this action dozens (if not hundreds) of times, I turned and said the axiom that inspired the title of this book (you'll have to read the story to know exactly what that was). Of course, we laughed once I said it, but later, while she was consumed by the Depression glass, I kept thinking about how fantastic it would be for a cosmetic company to use my words as an advertising slogan.

After legally protecting the catchphrase and campaign design, I put together a presentation without giving *all* of the details away. I contacted anyone and everyone I knew in the cosmetic and advertising industries (reputable or otherwise) and immediately hit a wall by consistently hearing, "If you bring this to a big or small advertising agency, and since you're not an employee…they'll steal it. Plain and simple. And if you bring it to a cosmetic company, they'll either steal it, or they'll tell you to go to the advertising agency they pay millions to annually for slogans and campaigns like yours...and they'll steal it." I was experiencing a Catch 22 without even enlisting.

Sure to get screwed from one company or another, I decided to take the advertising concept, along with my education of Depression glass, and put them into the memory vault...hoping one day I'd be able to use them.

And now I have...well, except for the Depression glass.

I hope you'll enjoy reading As Long As I Have Lips as much as I enjoyed writing it.

The names in this romantic-comedy have been made up, or they've been taken randomly from my phonebook...and they're not intended to be, in any way, conducive to the characters they may portray in this fictional story.

I use *italics* and ellipses (such as: ...). Why? Because that's the way we speak! They are there to alter the way you read.

Italics *emphasize* the specific word.

Ellipses are used as a timing rest...while staying on the same subject.

The italics and ellipses make the reading of this story more enjoyable and bring the characters to life.

As usual, I've included a Cast of Characters (in order of their appearance) at the end...just in case you need to reference it from time-to-time.

Oh, and if those last six paragraphs sound familiar...check out THE BOSS *ALWAYS* SITS IN THE BACK, DEADFELLAS and THE DELIVERY MAN.

Enjoy!

CHAPTER 1
Jeffrey Holland Was On A Mission

Working for a prestigious New York City advertising agency was all Jeffrey Holland ever wanted. It was his dream. It was his goal… and he had attained it at twenty-four.

New York City's weather on Monday, May 6th, 2019 was exceptionally pleasant. It had rained all weekend, so as Jeffrey stepped from the R train and up the concrete steps two-at-a-time from the 7th Avenue and West 57th Street subway station, the air at 8:42AM was fresh and clean…by Manhattan's standards. Jeffrey loved his job so much that in the five months since leaving Montana and moving to "the City," he never cared *what* the weather conditions were like.

Dressed in one of his neatly pressed suits, Jeffrey carried a soft leather briefcase via a strap over his right shoulder as he made his way through the normal hustle-and-bustle of a weekday morning. Similarly clad male and female junior executives carried briefcases, wore backpacks, sipped lattes or guzzled coffee, listened to whatever audio app they subscribed to with the tiniest of earpads, and talked or texted into phones as they scurried in every direction to be at their desks by 9AM.

Jeffrey often varied his path from the subway station to *his* junior executive office on the 44th floor of the Time Warner Center's South Tower. When short on time, he'd hurry west on West 57th, turn north along Broadway, then west onto West 58th Street for one block, cross 8th Avenue and make his way into the massive structure via the 58th Street entrance at the base of the South Tower. When he had extra time and wanted to enjoy a walk along the southern edge of Central Park, he'd emerge from the subway and head north on 7th Avenue to the curved 18 floor apartment building at 200 Central Park South, then make a left to stroll along the park for one long block to Columbus Circle at the intersections of 8th Avenue, Broadway, West 59th Street and Central Park West, and enter the Center's 60th Street door.

In reality, the building itself wasn't important to Jeffrey. He was hired shortly after the beginning of the year by Arthur, O'Connell & Ruppert, a stalwart advertising agency of Madison Avenue since 1973, and known as AOR. They relocated to the South Tower in 2003.

Today the handsome, 5'8, Rocky Mountain-homegrown junior executive was a little rushed…so he took the direct route. His stride made it easy for all to see that Jeffrey was on a mission. He wasn't looking up at the skyscrapers as he normally would, nor did he admire the women that walked toward him…not even the ones who smiled. Cars, trucks, buses, taxis and messengers on bicycles passed without Jeffrey giving them a second thought.

Somewhere on 58th Street between Broadway and 8th Avenue he took out his phone, tapped a pre-programmed number and started talking as soon as he heard a voice.

"Okay, I'm above ground." Ever the gentleman, he said, "Please continue with what you were saying. Are you *sure* they dumped Carter and Brown?"

"Yes, sir," replied Rekha Vajpayee, Jeffrey's thirty-two-year-old Hindi accented assistant assigned to him when he got the job. She came with a downtown Manhattan attitude, along with its sense of humor and lexicon…and often blurted out the unexpected.

"When did you hear about it?"

"Last night," Rekha quickly responded. "I was having drinks with my friend who works in Divine's Marketing Department," the assistant answered proudly.

As if doubting what she said, Jeffrey pressed, "Are you sure?"

"Their contract runs out at midnight tonight and Divine's owner told CB she's not renewing. They're--"

Jeffrey interrupted, "CB?"

"Carter and Brown," she answered and tried to hold back some laughter. "Anyway, they're keeping it quiet. My friend said he wasn't supposed to tell me, but the power of a few drinks and some cleavage has an amazing effect on a lot of men's ability to keep a secret."

"That's *another* reason why I don't drink," Jeffrey replied, embarrassed by hearing about his assistant's cleavage.

Knowing her openness had made him uncomfortable, Rekha resumed the conversation with, "What do you want to do about this, Mr. Holland?"

With all the confidence in the world, Jeffrey commanded, "I want the Divine account." He thought for a second and continued with, "Call the Art Director and ask them to have someone in my office in twenty minutes. I'll be there in ten."

With more volume than one would normally address a superior, Rekha blurted, "Don't you mean '*Tell them* to have someone here in twenty minutes'?"

Showing his inexperience and naiveté in the ways of Manhattan and the advertising world, Jeffrey sheepishly answered, "I don't want to upset the Art Director."

Rekha shot back, "*Upset?* You're worrying about pissing off the Art Director for an account like *Divine?* I thought this was *important* to you, boss."

He knew she was right. Not having acquired any semblance of a *City* attitude yet, he said, "Okay…do whatever you think is best."

With her sarcastic City demeanor and Hindi accent, Rekha retorted, "They'd better *not* give us any shit about it. This could be the biggest account--" Again she realized what she had said, then tried to apologize for it with, "Oh, I'm sorry, Mr. Holland. Sometimes those words just come out."

Though taken aback by Rekha's cursing, he told her, "It's okay. It's only because you're as excited as I am about the Divine account. Get someone up there and let's see what we can come up with."

"Yes, Mr. Holland. I'll get right on it."

"And Rekha…"

"Yes?"

"How many times do I have to tell you?"

"Yes…*Jeff*. I'll see you in a little bit."

Within seconds of hanging up, Jeffrey approached a bus stop enclosure on the corner of 8th Avenue displaying several advertisements. It was the one depicting a model applying red lipstick with the bold red lettered slogan, "*Divine Cosmetics…Like Kissing A Fantasy!*" that made him smile and walk faster.

Jeffrey was proud that he had learned the advertising industry's history in New York City.

No one could ever deny that New York City's borough of Manhattan was the birthplace of the "advertising industry," which became known by the island's multi-lane artery that runs north from 23rd Street to 142nd Street along the city's grid, and named for America's fourth President, James Madison.

As the number of the nation's newspapers increased in the second half of the 1800s, especially with several dailies in New York City alone, the need for *slogan factories* proliferated, causing the industry of advertising to blossom.

During the 20th Century's first quarter, as early skyscrapers made their way uptown, the pioneering "advertising agencies" claimed the avenue as their territory and made the term "Madison Avenue" synonymous with their industry. It began with the promotions of local events and products, then precipitously grew into national print and radio ads.

Every housewife wanted to know what to buy as she listened to the magic box in the living room, and the mighty men of the advertising industry were happy to supply her with commercials ranging from the cigarettes her husband wanted to smoke and the shirts he needed to wear, to the soap she'd need to wash the kids *and* their clothes.

The one product ad agencies determined sold best with the "stay at home" demographic was soap.

Soap by every manufacturer, of every variety and for every use…as long as they could afford the agency's fees and broadcaster's rates. The result spawned the never-ending stream of advertisements on radio and television shows that gave birth to its own genre, the "Daytime Soap Opera"…30-minute serialized dramas each happy homemaker could relate to while her husband was at work, their kids were in school, the clothes were drying outside on the line…and every 8.5 minutes there would be a 120-second set of four commercials telling her everything she needed to put on the household shopping list.

And she obediently did it.

But it was when the wonderful world of television erupted across North America in the early 1950s that Madison Avenue became the road paved with gold.

It wasn't long before America's population became obsessed and looked forward to commercials showcasing the new car models released every September for the following year. In 1955, the Volkswagen Beetle was introduced to America for $1,050, and Cadillac sold its convertible Coupe deVille for $4,400. The country's new highway system was crisscrossing the continent as consumers were told by song to *"See the USA in your Chevrolet!"*

In natural succession the next fad to inundate the public were the endless miles of billboards that peppered the highways, freeways, parkways and turnpikes. Burma Shave, Howard Johnson's, Stuckey's, Dairy Queen, there were thousands of them, whether nationally known companies or local Mom & Pop diners…each was designed to entertain, inform and entice every vehicle's occupants as they cruised by at 60 miles an hour. This was all in conjunction with endless TV, radio and print ads for gasoline companies whose neatly uniformed, cap-wearing, always smiling Caucasian attendant would check the air in your tires, the oil in your engine and clean your windshield while filling the car's tank with fuel at 29 cents a gallon…all sucked from the ground and processed from the oil fields of America.

By the 1960s, fashion, music, alcohol, film and tobacco companies had realized that spending a couple of million dollars to promote their products would result in a rapid return in the *hundreds* of millions.

It also didn't take long for political parties to realize the value of having Madison Avenue work for them. From images of a candidate's wholesome, god-worshipping, clean cut family to nuclear devastation…advertising was to become *the* primary factor in determining election outcomes.

By the 1970s, cars, beer cans, liquor bottles, airlines, cereal boxes, fashion, soup cans, remote and exotic vacation locations, *everything* was appearing as "subliminal product placement" in TV shows and feature films. Everything America saw, heard, smelled, ate, drank, voted for, cleaned with, smoked, read, traveled to, wore or drove had Madison Avenue's hands in it. There was no limit to what they could or would promote.

Early in the game, the advertising boys found one essential factor to be more effective than anything else in selling whatever product they were contracted to publicize…and they never stopped using it.

If anything, they consistently improved on the endless ways to exploit it.

Sex.

Sex sells.

Beginning in the 1950s, the more an advertisement showed attractive, enticing women exposing skin or cooing a double-entendre, or a dashing well-dressed man smoking a pipe and holding a martini as he stood next to his new home and car…the more that product sold and stayed in the minds of the consumer.

Men *wanted* the woman in the ad, and women wanted to *be* the woman in the ad. At least that's what was subliminally being put into the minds of the public.

There was no stopping Madison Avenue. And the bigger the industry became, the more money flowed into its agencies' coffers… and the coffers of their clients.

That was all that mattered.

Then came the Digital Age in the early 1990s…and things began to change.

Drastically.

The age, race and sex of the up-and-comers went through a transformation. Madison Avenue had always been a *Straight White Man's Domain* where college graduates would spend several years in apprenticeship under an agency's "elders" before being allowed to present a campaign to a client.

Suddenly, men and women in their twenties of all cultures and sexual orientations were looked to for the slogans and campaigns that would lead the industry into the next century.

In addition, unlike the 'old school' crew, this new generation knew how to work in the embryonic and rapidly growing world of computer technology and the internet.

It wasn't long before the memories of "three-martini lunches" in The Oak Room Bar at The Plaza Hotel were all that remained of the once ruling agencies of Madison Avenue.

The companies that didn't merge or go out of business were absorbed by conglomerates and relocated into home offices across the country…or to another continent entirely. For some, the rents of Madison Avenue were their demise, so they moved downtown into the trendy, re-gentrified and less expensive buildings of Tribeca, the West Village and the Flatiron District.

A few of the older agencies enlisted young talent and relocated into the new addresses of Midtown Manhattan, such as the majestic twin-towered, 55 floor Time Warner Center erected on the four-and-a-half-acre site of the famous New York Coliseum that once stood on the west side of Columbus Circle from 1956 to 2000, spanning from 58th to 60th Street, and 8th Avenue halfway down to 9th Avenue.

The Time Warner Center opened its doors for business in 2003, resulting in a few longtime Madison Avenue agencies to quickly move in. Arthur, O'Connell & Ruppert was one of them…and Jeffrey had made it to these offices despite his unlikely background with those he now worked.

A little more than an hour after Jeffrey Holland had hung up with Rekha, a white stretch limousine crawled south on 5th Avenue and approached a red light at East 58th Street. Cars, trucks, buses and taxis surrounded the limo. Everything was at a standstill…except for an abundance of female pedestrians who were hurrying to cross the street. A few went as far as jaywalking around the stopped vehicles.

It took a mere second to realize the inordinate number of women of every age, ethnicity, shape, size and wardrobe, risking injury as they all headed to the same place…Bergdorf Goodman, one of 5th Avenue's upscale stores that cater to the rich…and the *very* rich.

Television trucks from the usual networks and NYC stations were parked at the entrance with camera crews filming the feminine influx. Something was going on.

In the backseat of the six-passenger white stretch sat Whitney Quinn.

Whitney didn't merely look like she was born to *sit* in the back of a limo, but thirty-three years earlier she was *born* in the back of one. With the raised partition separating her and her longtime driver,

Whitney, more than attractive, with fashionably styled light-brown hair and eyeglasses, contemporary jewelry, a statuesque 5'10, dressed for business, was giving her best 'over the phone voice of sincerity' to her date from Friday night to Saturday afternoon.

"I'm telling you, Vance…it *was* fun, but it's Monday and I can't do dinner. I'm busy the whole week, so how about I call you--"

The commotion of those crossing the street distracted Whitney, especially once she noticed they were women…and *only* women.

Returning her attention to the phone, she dropped the sincerity act and switched to her normal business tone, "Vance, I'll let you know when something opens up. I gotta go," then disconnected the call.

Just as the traffic light turned green she pressed the button to lower the passenger side window for a better view of the goings on as the limo crawled across 58th Street and past Bergdorf's entrance.

A look of pain gripped Whitney's face as she turned her neck to the right to eye the TV trucks. That was when a NYC Transit bus crept alongside the limo and blocked her view. Raising the window, she caught the large ad on the side of the bus that showed two beautiful models holding bottles of perfume with the bold blue letters of its slogan, "*Judian…You Deserve It*," below them.

The limo's window completed its slide to the top as Whitney rubbed an ache on the right side of her neck, then flipped her head from right to left hoping for something to pop. But nothing did. Opening the vanity mirror above her head, she pulled a tube of lipstick from her purse, applied it, admired the look and gave herself a smile.

No sooner did she put the lipstick away and close the mirror when her phone rang.

Eyeing the Caller ID to see the name "James Dorsett," she didn't think twice before saying "Shit" under her breath, then tapped the Ignore button and tossed the phone on the seat next to her.

Lowering the partition, she asked her fifty-nine-year old driver, "Stuart, is there a reason you didn't turn on Sixtieth Street?"

"Road construction down to Seventh Avenue all week, Miss Quinn" came from the trusted driver. "I'll turn on Fifty-Seventh and you'll be there in about fifteen or twenty minutes."

Living in a 31st floor apartment of The Pierre, an elite Manhattan residence at the corner of 5th Avenue and East 61st Street, Whitney was shuttled daily by Stuart in the limo owned by the company where she worked. It rarely took more than 20 minutes of normal city traffic to get to her office, though today would take a little longer and there was nothing she could do but leave it to the man who had been her personal driver for the last eight years. She sat back to enjoy the ride…but not before she gave the ache in her neck another rub and stretch as she wondered what was going on at Bergdorf's.

Women jammed each aisle leading to Bergdorf Goodman's Cosmetics Department to get to the Judian counters that were surrounded by lights, cameras, reporters and photographers.

Once Judian's publicist, Bergdorf's VP of Special Promotions, the Fire Marshall and most importantly the CEO of Evers & Glosson determined that not one more human body could fit, the stunningly beautiful and recognizable spokesmodel was given *the wink*. Walking into the lights, she approached the perfectly placed microphone above an exquisite two-tiered display of cosmetics and perfumes, then waved her hand above them and sighed through the speakers, "Judian's new line, because…*you deserve it*," then was led away by the publicist.

The crowd lost their minds in applause as equally beautiful models inched through the throng spraying and moisturizing women with the latest Judian products. Boxes and bags were being picked and purchased by the infatuated crowd as fast as salespeople could process their credit cards.

The TV cameras and photographers caught it all.

Evers & Glosson was the company that came up with the "*You Deserve It*" campaign several weeks earlier, causing their CEO and Bergdorf's VP of Special Promotions to have the biggest smiles in the store.

CHAPTER 2
"This Slogan Has Got To Be *Universal*"

Walking to the elevator bay servicing the 35th to 52nd floors, Jeffrey entered the first to open its doors. He pressed "44," stood with his back against the side wall and waited as the elevator filled with more junior executives and assistants.

The doors eventually opened into the lobby of Arthur, O'Connell & Ruppert, and as he did every day upon stepping out, he looked at the clock. It was 8:59. Jeffrey smiled, proud of the fact that since being hired, he had never arrived past nine o'clock.

It was common knowledge that the higher-ups didn't get in until ten or eleven, but Jeffrey had set strict rules for himself before going east…rules compiled and meant to keep him on the straight-and-narrow, and to uphold his promise to his mother, "…to not get taken in by the ways and women of New York City." Vowing not to drink anything stronger than beer was one of them. Being at the office before 9AM was another.

After checking the time, he and the receptionist had their daily exchange.

"Good morning, Nora," Jeffrey greeted her courteously.

Sitting at a large curved desk below the company's name in letters suspended from one side of the lobby to the other, sat Nora, mid-forties, employed by AOR for nearly two decades, and most of all…she was professional. Nora made the perfect first impression to any potential customer, whether coming into the lobby or on the telephone.

Wearing an earpiece, she raised her index finger signaling Jeffrey to wait, tapped a button on the phone console in front of her and took an incoming call.

"Good morning, Arthur, O'Connell and Ruppert." Listening for a few seconds, Nora continued with an audible smile, "Thank you. Hold on and I'll connect you to her office."

She pressed two buttons, made eye contact with the younger man, smiled and said, "Good morning, Mr. Holland," then rolled her eyes, realizing the mistake she often made due to years of corporate programming, then giggled and corrected herself.

"Morning... *Jeff.*"

He gave his usual wink for such innocent errors, scanned his code-key into the reader and opened the door leading to AOR's inner-offices.

The white limo drove to the Time Warner Center's 58th Street entrance at 10:27AM. Stuart opened the driver's side passenger door and without a word, Whitney breezed out. Striding into the building, she went to the same elevator bay Jeffrey had walked to.

She chose the closest of the three available and hit "52." Once the doors closed she rubbed her neck and now her right shoulder. As they opened into Dorsett & Mathers' lobby, a weeping woman in her forties, carrying a cardboard box full of personal possessions one would find in an executive's office, walked in. Two earpiece-wearing gorillas from Security followed her. Whitney didn't give the scene a second thought as she stepped out so the guards could pass.

Once out of the elevator, she bolted toward the door leading to the executive offices, wanting to avoid eye contact with Tania, the twenty-five-year old receptionist who also wore an earpiece and expertly tapped buttons on the console before her. Behind Tania was a mural bearing the company's logo.

"Good morning, Dorsett and Mathers Advertising," she competently responded to a call. After listening, the receptionist said, "Hold on and I'll connect you." She transferred the call, then said to the passing executive, "Good morning, Miss Quinn!"

Almost making it to the door that would have separated them, Whitney stopped in her tracks. She had to respond.

"Morning…uhm…"

"Tania."

"Morning, Tania."

The receptionist held up two messages and said, "Mr. Dorsett called twice. He said to call the beach house."

It was obvious this wasn't something Whitney wanted to deal with at that moment.

"Does Adam have my messages?" the executive asked.

"I'm sure he does, Miss Quinn. But these came through the front desk, not your office line. I asked if he wanted to be transferred to Adam or your voicemail, but Mr. Dorsett said he wanted me to get to you before you got to your desk. Sorry."

Letting out a sigh, Whitney sympathetically looked at the receptionist and apologetically said, "Thank you, Tania," then scanned her code-key, made her way inside and walked the hallway, eventually reaching the elaborate double-doors with a gold plaque in the center that read, "Whitney Quinn – Vice President."

Having gotten the call from Tania that his boss was on the way, Adam Bryant, Whitney's highly-efficient, twenty-seven-year old black assistant, arrived just before she did to push the doors open for her to enter. The automatic lights turned on as he followed her with a legal pad at his side. There was a cool, relaxed side to Adam's corporate voice, clothes and mannerism that Whitney liked.

"Did you call to make sure he'd be here?" the boss asked as she made a bee-line to the walk-in closet in the massive corner office that was filled with stylish corporate furniture, contemporary artwork, framed magazine covers and Clio awards for international advertising campaigns. The floor-length curtains that covered the converging walls were closed.

"On Friday," Adam nonchalantly responded as he closed the doors behind them.

She disappeared into the walk-in closet that included a private bathroom and shower, leaving the door ajar and continued their conversation with, "I see another head rolled this morning."

As Adam perused the list of items on that day's agenda, he replied, "She spent too much on presentations, meals, drinks, *more* presentations, focus groups, the usual…and couldn't get the client to bite, so they went elsewhere. It was one of those power drink companies." He let out a sigh and finished with, "Such is life in the world of advertising, ladies and gentlemen."

Whitney rubbed the ache in her neck and shoulder before slipping off her heels. She scanned the closet's two tiers of casual and dress clothes on hangers, a few shelves of workout gear, drawers of jewelry and eyeglasses, a selection of jackets and coats, a vanity with drawers of make-up, and an array of footwear. Beginning to undress, she called out, "Okay Adam…hit me."

He sat in a chair outside the closet and called back, "Messages from Friday? Office gossip? Or who's looking for a new agency?"

"Gossip."

"McCoslin…Director of Personnel…" Adam responded.

She sarcastically retorted, "The guy who never smiles and reeks of cigarettes. I was never sure how he got that job. What about him?"

"Security caught his daughter doin' a custodian in daddy's office over the weekend…again."

Whitney's head peeked around the door and asked with concern, "Again?"

"What can I tell you? She's got a thing for getting nailed on her father's desk. Don't ask me, 'cause I don't get it. I mean, I can see doin' it in the office, but not with any of the custodial staff. Apparently, it's her boyfriend. McCoslin hired him a month ago."

Adam heard his boss chuckle as she slipped on a chenille robe, tied the belt, then swung the closet door open. With her feet encased in fur-lined slippers, she shuffled across the room. None of it affected Adam because there was nothing unusual about this for a Monday morning.

Reaching the desk placed between the corner windows, she sat in her custom-fitted high-back leather chair, stretched her neck and said, "Management shouldn't be allowed to hire family...but that's just *my* opinion. Remind me to talk to Dorsett about that."

Adam relocated to a leather chair facing Whitney's desk, efficiently wrote her command on the pad with his Mont Blanc Gold-Coated Classique, then said, "Talking about Dorsett--"

"Yeah, I know. Later for that...anything else about the daughter? Did her father fire her?"

"He couldn't," came Adam's response, offhandedly.

Whitney, a twinge of anger in her voice, asked "Why the fuck not?" as she began looking through a stack of the latest issues of *Elle*, *Allure*, *Glamour*, *Vogue* and *Harper's Bazaar*.

"She's not an employee," Adam answered.

Whitney barked, "And she has a *code-key?*"

Adam shook his head and answered, "Security said it was her father's. Therein lies the problem."

Leaning back in her chair with a copy of *Glamour* in her hands, Whitney was ready to move on.

"Next."

Adam asked, "Business? Or messages from Friday?"

"Messages...and when is he getting here?"

"Any minute. Relax." Adam's eyes scrolled down the pad and read, "A Vance called to confirm dinner at eight. He didn't leave a last name. Said you'd know. I assume you went."

"The Skylark. He had no idea it was my third time there this month. But those were for business. This was a date. I like a rooftop view, but Thirty-ninth between Seventh and Eighth? Really? Me? For a date?" She flipped through the magazine's pages and vented. "If he took the time to ask, or to even *Google* me for Christ-sake, he'd know I don't like being in public. I prefer to see the City from Brooklyn or Jersey. I wanna *see* the skyline, not be part of it. I had my fill of 'City places' since I came back from college."

"Vance?" Adam pressed.

"An Ashton Seafood heir. Third generation. *Very* handsome," she said, then put down the magazine, picked up *Vogue* and laughed, "And seafood? I doubt he's ever been on the water in anything other than his family's yacht."

Adam chuckled, but said nothing…knowing she had more to say. Scanning the magazine's pages, Whitney didn't miss a beat and kept going.

"Manners and intelligence? He gets a six. Did I mention he was very handsome?"

"Yes."

Whitney held back laughter as she continued with, "Then he *really* tanked with whatever that was he served for coffee on Saturday morning," and followed it with a *yuck* face.

Raising his head from the pad, he queried, "Saturday morning?"

"I mentioned that he was handsome, right?"

Now it was Adam holding back the laughter, then asked, "So?" with his pen to the pad. He jotted down her statement as soon as she began speaking.

"When he calls…and he will…tell him I had to go out of town. Next."

"We need to discuss the three calls from Mr. Dorsett," Adam interjected, pushing their assumed urgency. "The last one came about ten minutes before you got here. He wants you to call him at--"

The boss interrupted, finishing Adam's sentence, "The beach house." She put the *Vogue* on top of the *Glamour*, picked up *Harper's Bazaar* and began scanning specific pages to view the ads of D&M's clients, then finally got to business with, "What was that about a company looking for a new agency?"

The assistant rose from his chair, walked behind Whitney's desk, picked up *Vogue*, thumbed through a dozen pages, found what he wanted and laid the open page in front of her.

She was looking at a model applying red lipstick, and the bold red lettered slogan that read, "*Divine Cosmetics...Like Kissing A Fantasy!*" Whitney raised her head *and* an eyebrow.

"What are you saying?"

Adam proudly replied, "It hasn't hit the streets yet, but Divine dumped Carter and Brown, and--"

Shocked, Whitney's *City* attitude came out, "Don't fuck with me, Adam."

"And they're looking for a new slogan," he retorted, completing his sentence.

He grabbed *Glamour*, went through some pages and held up the ad of two beautiful models holding bottles of perfume with the bold blue letters of the slogan, "*Judian...You Deserve It*," below them.

"Judian's new lines, along with their new faces and slogan just came out...and it's *hot*. They had a big event at Bergdorf's this morning."

Whitney interjected, saying, "And Divine's looking for something new to compete with them." Shaking her head, she added, "It makes sense, but I never thought she'd change that slogan."

Returning the magazine atop the desk, Adam asked, "Why not?"

Whitney leaned her head back, looked at the ceiling and answered, "Long story, Adam. You don't wanna know."

After a few seconds of thinking, but still looking up, she told Adam, as his pen was poised on the pad anticipating her instructions,

"Call Divine. Get me a meeting with Gail Burrelle. Tonight. For dinner. Anywhere. Her choice." He nodded, and she continued, "We'll hit her top money-maker. Get the Art Department started on lipstick designs. No slogans. Don't tell them who it's for. I want a tight lock on this. No one is to know we're going after Divine… especially anyone working *here*." The Classique wrote her every word. "I'll start working on slogan ideas after lunch. I want something to show Burrelle *tonight*." Then Whitney lowered her head, rubbed her neck and shoulders, looked at Adam and asked, "And where the fuck is my mass--"

There was a knock on the door.

Adam didn't miss a beat, grinned and answered, "Voila," as he rose, made his way to the double-doors and opened them.

A tall, muscular, blonde male carrying a cushioned folding-table entered. He smiled at Whitney. She smiled back.

There was no longer a need for Adam to be in the room, so with the pad at his side he walked out and closed the door behind him as the masseur set up the table in front of the curtained windows. Whitney tapped a button on her desk causing the curtains to part, revealing a breathtaking view of the southern end of Central Park, all the way across town to the East River.

Eight floors below, Jeffrey Holland vigorously paced around his office. It was a small room decorated with the standard furniture and wall dressings of a junior executive. The brass nameplate on the door read his name, followed by "Account Executive."

Jeffrey's diploma from Montana State University and two awards from the Rocky Mountain Association of Advertising Agencies hung on the wall behind his faux-leather chair. The window overlooked rusty water towers atop the apartment buildings from 8th Avenue to 10th, and south to the Port Authority Bus Terminal. The analog clock on the wall showed 10:59. The room was overrun with poster boards of art designs, storyboards, donuts, coffee cups, and a variety of Divine Cosmetics lipstick tubes scattered around.

"It's close, Paige. But it needs more. It's got to be the ultimate slogan. *That's* what we need," Jeffrey excitedly said to the graphic artist assigned to the project. He walked behind his desk and sat facing Paige and his assistant Rekha. It was easy for them to see how much he loved his job and what he was doing.

Placed prominently on his desk was a framed 8x10 photograph of a ten-year-old Jeffrey sitting on a tractor…in the lap of a woman in her mid-thirties. His mother. She wore overalls, work gloves and boots, with sweat on her brow…and affectionately held her son.

Rekha and Paige held up posters of large pairs of lips. One had lips coated in pink with the words *"Divine Cosmetics Pink Dreams."* The other had shiny red lips with the text, *"Divine Cosmetics Red Erotica."*

They didn't work.

Jeffrey, with passion in his voice and hand gestures, said, "It's… it's got to be something *everyone* can relate to! One great slogan that will change the world!"

Rekha blurted out, "Of all of Divine's products, lipstick is number one, Mr. Holland! You think you can come up with something--" she caught her mistake and continued, "Sorry…Jeff. You think you can come up with something better than…" she broke into her best sexual voice, *"Divine Lipstick. Like Kissing A Fantasy,"* then got serious and kept going, "They've been using that forever, and new slogans, *great* new slogans don't happen overnight."

Jeffrey was on a mission and shot back with, "Until Judian's *'You Deserve It'* came along."

Rekha held her ground with, "And *that* took Evers and Glosson months to come up with."

He wasn't going to let that stop him and commanded the subordinates to set up a 3 o'clock focus group. "We'll see what the public thinks," he said with confidence.

The women were stunned. They had never known of someone in Jeffrey's position to take such a chance…at least not someone who wanted to keep their job if it failed.

He took Paige's poster in his hand and said, "This slogan has got to be *universal*."

The artist asked, "And that means…?"

The Account Executive took some time before articulately answering.

"After seeing or hearing it *just once*…everyone…every man and woman regardless of where they are…will know exactly what the product is and who made it. It's an advertising concept made for one world. *That* is universal."

"And what *is* that slogan, Mr. Holland?" Paige pressed.

Rekha corrected her, "Jeff."

Her boss smiled and they exchanged winks.

"Jeff," added Paige.

"I'll be honest," Jeffrey answered. "I have no idea…yet."

His assistant acerbically tossed in, "And you want a focus group at three?"

"Let's make the stakes even higher, Rekha," Jeffrey said, which resulted in both women looking concerned. "Just like I do, Divine's CEO believes advertising a product is *all about the slogan*. Get me a meeting with Gail Burrelle tonight…for dinner. If we can put something together fast enough, *and* if I can get Mr. Ruppert to approve it, we can nab the Divine account. I *know* it."

Speaking her mind, Paige said with conviction, "If you want mock-ups by three. I'm gonna need that universal slogan pretty fuckin' soon."

Jeffrey was stunned and went silent.

Rekha's eyebrows rose and looked at the graphic artist, knowing her boss wasn't accustomed to women using such language. She changed the subject as fast as she could with, "Jeff, what do you say we postpone the focus group and the meeting with Burrelle for a day or two? I know you're the new guy and you want to show the bosses they're getting their money's worth, but coming up with 'the perfect slogan' in a couple of hours for such a big account…it could backfire on you. It could backfire on *all* of us."

Leaning across his desk toward the women, the zeal of this project was evident from the gleam in his eyes and the certainty in his voice as he told them, "By now, the top agencies in the country have heard the news, and each one wants this account as bad as I do. But I'm telling you, there's no one who wants it *more*. I bet there's someone right now, probably right here in this building, thinking the exact…same…thing."

As Jeffrey spoke those impressive words in his junior executive office, eight floors above him came the erotic moans of, "*Ohhh yeeeeaaahhhh!*" and "*Oooohhh! Right fuckin' there!*"

They were oozing from Whitney Quinn, face down on the masseur's table. Her head was buried in a lavender scented towel, her naked body was covered by a sheet, her nose and lips were visible through the hole in the face pillow, and the music of Patrick O'Hearn emitted from hidden speakers.

"*Don't you stop. Please don't you stop,*" she murmured as the masseur worked on the kinks in her right shoulder and neck. Whitney knew how to go with the pain and let out a deep, "*Aaaaaaahhhh,*" as she felt him massage the tight muscles.

"A lot on your mind, Miss Executive?" he asked, as if they had been doing this for years…which they had.

"Business. It's *always* business. But at the moment, it's cosmetics. Lipstick, primarily," Whitney answered through the hole.

"Sorry. Can't help you," he replied truthfully. "Organic body oils? I got you covered. Lipstick? Outta my realm," then he tapped her on the shoulder letting her know it was time to turn over.

As she rotated and moved down a little so he could remove the face pillow, Whitney said with determination, "Yeah, but not outta mine."

Once she was comfortable, the masseur stood behind her head and used his strong, capable hands to massage and manipulate the muscles in her neck, then gently turned and stretched it. Everything adjusted itself as she heard the pops and cracks, then felt the release of the weekend's tightness disappear…causing Whitney to melt into the table.

CHAPTER 3
How It All Started

Adam diligently worked at his computer as he noticed the clock in the bottom corner go to 12:06PM. That was also the moment Whitney, very relaxed from her massage and shower, stepped from her office into his work area. The assistant was deep into whatever he was typing, so he didn't look up to see her wearing a dark brunette wig topped with a Nick Fouquet Crystal Mist Fur Felt Fedora and dressed for business. He raised his head to ask, "Did you call Mr. Dorsett?"

As Whitney dug into her Coach Signature Shoulder Bag, she answered, "Don't worry about Dorsett," then changed the subject. "I'm going to Saks, Bloomies and Bergdorf's to check out the cosmetic counters. I've got to come up with a slogan and that may be where some inspiration will hit."

As Adam returned to his typing he nonchalantly asked, "And the wig?"

Still rummaging through the purse, Whitney explained, "I'm incognito. I don't want anyone to know I'm there." Finding what she was searching for, she pulled out a dark pair of Tom Ford sunglasses, slipped them on and ran her hand through the fake locks of hair.

Just before she stepped away from his desk, Adam informed his boss, "You have dinner at seven-thirty with Gail Burrelle at The Palm Steakhouse."

"Tribeca or West Side?" she asked, clearly hoping for one over the other.

"West Side. Eight blocks away. After putting your presentation together, I thought it would be too tight for you to get downtown. I offered the closer one and her assistant agreed. You lucked out."

Not too thrilled with the menu at The Palm, Whitney complained...in Italian, "Bistecca?"

Confused, Adam responded, "Huh?" Then he remembered, "Oh, I forgot," he laughed as he looked at her schedule on his monitor, "You're in Italian mode. You're tutor comes at two." Recalling where they left off, Adam suggested, "So don't have the steak...have lobster."

"Ah...aragosta! Grazie," she happily said and began the walk to the lobby.

Down on the 44th floor, Rekha was in her cubicle outside of Jeffrey's office typing into her computer, which showed 12:08PM in the bottom corner. Her boss approached looking stressed.

"Raye, I'm going to take a walk...maybe up Madison Avenue."

Rekha stopped what she was doing, eyed the time and then looked up to ask him, with more than a little concern in her voice, "*Now? There?* Why?"

Jeffrey's response was tinged with hope.

"For some inspiration. Madison Avenue was where the original Divine slogan came from. I'm willing to try anything right about now."

In her quick, no-nonsense tone, just before Jeffrey was about to step away, she barked, "Well, you'd better come up with something, boss...and it better be good! Your focus group is set for three, and you're having breakfast with Burrelle at nine tomorrow morning in The Palm Court at The Plaza."

His eyebrows shot up. Before he could ask, "How did you do that so fast?" Rekha returned her attention to typing and offhandedly said, "It's what good assistants do. I almost snagged dinner tonight, but someone with a little more juice got to her first."

Giving her a thumbs-up and amused by her choice of words, Jeffrey now had the stress of a focus group in less than three hours, not having a slogan or artwork, and breakfast with Gail Burrelle to think about as he walked away.

Passing through the lobby, Jeffrey waved to Nora as he strode past the receptionist's desk toward the elevator. It was only a few seconds before the bell chimed and the doors parted.

Stepping inside, he saw the lone fedora-wearing brunette, her eyes covered by sunglasses and sensuously sliding red lipstick across her lips.

Jeffrey respectfully smiled at her and nodded, but she didn't notice.

With more important things on his mind, he turned and hit the already lit 'Lobby' button. The doors closed. There was nothing for Jeffrey to do but watch the floor numbers decline.

Whitney finished applying the lipstick, but as she opened her purse, the lipstick tube slipped from her hand and dropped to the floor.

Jeffrey turned, then quickly and gentlemanly knelt to pick it up. "Allow me."

Sweetly, Whitney replied, "Grazie, grazie."

Assuming she didn't speak English, as Jeffrey stood he slowly said, "Excuse me, but...you have a very beautiful smile..." then he pointed to her mouth, and continued with, "...and great lips."

Staying in character, the advertising executive innocently smiled at his hand gesture and answered, "Ah, grazie. Lei e' molto gentile'."

Eyeing the lipstick tube as he handed it to her, and figuring she had no clue as to what he was saying, he nonchalantly said, "I guess as long as women have lips...they'll have lipstick."

Jeffrey realized *the best slogan of his life* had just hit him.

Whitney was about to say something, but even she stopped to think about what she had just heard.

The elevator doors opened into the lobby.

The only thing on Jeffrey's mind was to get back to his office... and it showed.

Not wanting to appear rude, he looked at the brunette and thought hard to remember the Italian translation of what he wanted to say, then spurted out, "Ahhh...arrivederci!" and left the elevator.

Jeffrey Holland was on a mission.

Whitney, with her mind racing, offhandedly threw out, "Si, ciao!"

Jeffrey walked into the next open elevator, pressed '44' and watched the doors close.

Whitney hadn't budged. She hit '52' and leaned against the wall...thinking.

Before the elevator doors could close, a young corporate male and female walked in.

Swiftly holding out her hand to block them, Whitney commanded with an authoritative and bitchy voice, "Get the next one, kids. This one's taken."

The woman, equally bitchy and obviously not aware of who Whitney was, shot back, "Get your hand out of my face. This elevator's empty!"

The couple turned to face the button panel. Just as the woman reached to press one, Whitney centered herself between them, put her hands on their backs, and said, "And empty is just the way I want it," then pushed them out as the doors closed.

The elevator rose.

Whitney Quinn was on a mission.

Simultaneously in their respective offices, Jeffrey and Whitney rushed to their assistants' desks. Within seconds Adam and Rekha picked up their phones to summon those who were needed.

Adam was given an extra command as Whitney took off her sunglasses, hat and wig while striding into her office, "Cancel my tutor!"

And he did.

CHAPTER 4
"So, Show Me What You've Got"

The white stretch pulled in front of 250 West 50th Street, timed perfectly so that when Stuart opened the door for Whitney to stride out and step into The Palm Steakhouse, it would be exactly 7:15PM. Fifteen minutes before the scheduled meeting.

Of course, passersby stopped to ogle the beautiful woman emerge from the limo's backseat attired from neck-to-toe in a Tory Burch ensemble. Whitney's chauffeur tipped his cap and bowed his head as she confidently entered the eatery holding a portfolio under her arm.

The next morning, with eight minutes to spare, the freshly polished shoes of Jeffrey Holland completed the quick walk from the 59th Street & 5th Avenue subway station to The Plaza's front door. Wearing his best suit and tie, with the soft leather briefcase slung over his left shoulder, the nervous junior executive was pointed toward The Palm Court restaurant.

Upon telling the maître d' his name, Jeffrey was led to the lavish table where Gail Burrelle was already seated and enjoying a glass of champagne.

Since the mid-1980s the name "Gail Burrelle" had been known by the patriarchy of Madison Avenue as "One sly, tough, sexy broad no one can get *anything* over on." Very attractive at sixty-three and standing five-feet-ten, Gail had always been a combination of class, balls, sexuality and an all-business attitude. Her attire that day was equivalent in style and designer to Whitney's from the previous evening.

Upon seeing Jeffrey's extended hand and hearing him clearly articulate, "Good morning, Miss Burrelle. I'm Jeffrey Holland from Arthur, O'Connell and Ruppert. Thank you for agreeing to have breakfast with me. It's a pleasure to meet you," Gail, still seated, was seductively looking the home-grown twenty-four-year old from Montana over. She smiled, took his hand and returned, "Very nice to meet *you*, Mr. Holland. Would you mind if I call you Jeffrey?"

The question stunned him for a few seconds.

"Of course," he replied, knowing it was the only thing he could say where he wouldn't embarrass himself due to his noticeable nervousness.

Gail's smile widened slightly, but retained the seductive attitude. She responded, "Good. I hope you don't mind that I ordered for us." Jeffrey eyed the flute of champagne at his place setting as she continued, "So why don't you sit down and relax."

Once seated, he removed the iPad Pro from his briefcase. Three servers delivered two small portions of caviar, chopped eggs on small pieces of toasted French bread and a refill of Gail's champagne. Jeffrey had never seen caviar before, nor was he knowledgeable in the process of its consumption…and it showed on his face.

It was also evident to Gail and the servers.

Trying to play it cool, Jeffrey set up the tablet to face Gail, the woman holding his future in her hands. What he was also doing was observing her skill of the small spoon used to ladle the proper amount of black roe onto the chopped egg and toast, and how much of it to eat per bite. Then he watched her wash it down to clear her palate with the required quantity of champagne so that her taste buds were again ready to experience the unique, combined flavor.

Between Gail's first and second bite, she eyed the naïve man and got down to business.

"Jeffrey, if you did your homework and researched *anything* about me and my company, you're aware that my sole belief is that *everything* comes down to the slogan. Do you really think you have something new? Something better than the one I've been using since I started Divine back in the Eighties? Something that will blow Judian's new slogan to hell?"

Jeffrey's confidence came through more intense than when he told Rekha and Paige of his quest to win the Divine account.

"Miss Burrelle, you're not only going to be impressed with the slogan...but with the *entire* ad campaign."

Gail was quick to answer, "I've heard it all before, Jeffrey," then added a sexual tease to her voice, "So, show me what you've got..." She sensuously pointed to the device facing her and ended the sentence with, "...in there."

The double-entendre went right over the innocent Jeffrey's head. Gail assumed it was because he was nervous.

Jeffrey fired up the iPad to start the presentation while saying, "The fictitious names are to give you an idea of how we can promote Divine's products with famous and recognizable names and faces... if that's the direction you'd like to take."

The screen turned white. The lower section of a woman's face appeared. In the center of the screen her seductive lips had red lipstick covering them. In the screen's lower right corner the words *Red Erotica...by Divine* appeared.

Burrelle smiled.

Jeffrey smiled.

The model then cooed, "As long as I have lips...I'll have lipstick."

Burrelle raised an eyebrow. Suddenly, she was *very* interested.

In the lower left corner of the screen the words *Lips by Leigh Ann Miller* faded in just before the screen went to black.

Gail asked, "How long?"

"Fifteen seconds."

With her eyebrow still raised, Gail kept the pace up with, "Perfect. But it's the sa--"

Excited at what would appear next, he interrupted saying, "Watch! Watch!" and pointed to the iPad.

The screen again turned white. The lower section of an Asian woman's face with her lips covered in bright yellow lipstick was dead-center. In the lower right corner the words *Midnight Sun...by Divine* appeared.

The model whispered in Chinese, "Lu guo wo you lips...Wo jiu you lip-i-stick."

In the lower left corner the words *Lips by Michele Pan* faded in just as the screen went to black.

"Mandarin?" Gail probed.

Jeffrey proudly nodded.

Gail continued with, "Interesting visuals, Jeffrey. But...where did you get that slo--"

The still nervous-yet-excited ad man politely held up his index finger and again interrupted her.

"Hold on! I think you'll *really* like *this one*."

Grinning at his exuberance, the cosmetic executive returned her attention to the screen that revealed a new face and lips, and a different shade of lipstick. In the lower right corner the words *Sahara Purple...by Divine* appeared. The German model commanded, "So lange ich lippen habe...hab ich auch lippenstift."

In the lower left corner the words *Lips by Franka Mueller* appeared, then the screen faded to black.

"Yes, I like the concept *very* much, Jeffrey. But...that slo--" Gail again tried to say.

"Just one more, please, Miss Burrelle," Jeffrey politely interrupted, knowing this would be his only opportunity to sell her on his campaign. He desperately wanted her to see *everything* he had prepared.

Getting a little frustrated, Gail watched the screen turn white with another centered pair of lips wearing another shade of lipstick. In the lower right corner the words *Chianti…by Divine* appeared.

The model conveyed seductively in Italian, "Finche' avro' le labra…Avro' bisogno di un rosetto."

In the lower left corner the words *Lips by Vanessa Flora* appeared just before the screen faded to black.

Tapping the remote, Jeffrey turned off the iPad.

"Now?" Gail humorously asked.

"Now."

"The lips on the screen…the text in the corners…they're marvelous, Jeffrey. Using different faces and languages to say the same slogan…that's inspired!" were Gail's first words.

Jeffrey beamed, "We also have them in Spanish, Japanese, Cajun, Russian, Cantonese, Hindi, Polish…if you'd care to see--"

Now it was her turn to interrupt *him*.

"It's the slogan, Jeffrey…"

He beamed brighter at her words.

Then she continued with, "I've already been sold on it…"

His look changed to confusion.

"…by Whitney Quinn, the VP from Dorsett-and-Mathers. Last night over dinner at The Palm Steakhouse."

His look of confusion changed to shock as Gail proceeded.

"I wasn't thrilled with her visuals. But that slogan…*'As Long As I Have Lips, I'll Have Lipstick'*…who wouldn't fuckin' love *that?*"

Shocked even more at her language, Jeffrey held in any reaction.

Gail sat back and asked, "Why are you pitching the same slogan? I'm sure you've been around enough advertising people to know that's not ethical in the slightest." Then she took a bite of a caviar-covered piece of toast and a mouthful of champagne.

Trying not to stutter while keeping his thoughts together, Jeffrey got out, "But I…but…*I* came up with it! *Yesterday in the elevator!* I said it to this woman…this *Italian* woman who--"

Ding! The lightbulb above his head went on.

He signaled a server for the check and returned the iPad into the leather briefcase while saying to his guest, "I've got to get back to the office. How long will you be in town?"

"I'm leaving later today," she replied. "I'm flying to Sedona for three nights, and then to Los Angeles on Friday for a fundraiser that night, and to meet with a couple of agencies who want to pitch their ideas on Monday."

"How can I contact you?" he pressed.

"In Sedona, I'll be at The Palms Retreat...but off the grid. No phones, computers, nothing to connect one with the world. Seventy-two hours of input-deprivation while being massaged, wrapped, sauna'd, steamed, fed, pampered and massaged *again*. It'll be wonderful."

Seeing an obvious pattern, he asked, "And in L.A.?"

"At The Beverly Hills Hotel..." Observing the confused look on his face, she ended it with, "...in The Palm Bungalow." Then she delicately consumed the final spoonful of caviar atop the remaining chopped egg covered square of toast and washed it down with the last of her champagne while still seductively eyeing the young, flustered and confused junior executive.

"That's very interesting, Miss Burrelle. Last night, The Palm Steakhouse, this morning here at The Palm Court, The Palms Retreat in Sedona and The Palm Bungalow in Beverly Hills...if you don't mind me saying, it sounds like you have an interest in palm trees."

"Let's call it a recently acquired eccentricity, and eccentricities are acceptable when one achieves a certain level of maturity and wealth. Look, Jeffrey, I like your visual concept. But it's the slogan that sticks in the public's mind. So...if you can't resolve this with Miss Quinn, then--"

A pissed-off Jeffrey growled, "There is no *'if,'* Miss Burrelle. I'll resolve it."

With a sly grin, she told him, "It's going to be interesting to see how this plays out, Jeffrey. It's not going to be easy to top that slogan, and if no one dazzles me by next Tuesday…I'm signing with D-and-M. You have until then."

She rose from her seat, causing Jeffrey to stand. Upon shaking hands, her sultry voice returned as she parted with, "It was *very* nice to meet you, Jeffrey, and I *do* hope we see each other again."

Then she walked away.

The waiter approached and placed the bill in front of the junior executive. He looked at the total, then at his untouched serving of caviar, little pieces of chopped egg covered toast and flute of champagne…and shook his head.

CHAPTER 5
A Greenie

Jeffrey stood in the mammoth lobby of the Time Warner Center's South Tower and looked at his cell phone. It was 10:47AM. With his leather briefcase slung over his shoulder, he waited in the bay of elevators that travelled between the 35th to the 52nd floors, the same one he had disembarked from after his encounter with the Italian woman the day before.

Or so he *thought* she was Italian.

He studied each brunette that stepped on or off each vertical transporter. Those with and without hats. With and without sunglasses. With and without purses. By 12:04PM, and with the lunch hour beginning, Jeffrey was tired, leaning against the wall and having a hard time keeping track of all the women who fit those demographics.

As one set of doors parted, Adam exited and walked past the unknown Jeffrey. A few seconds later Rekha emerged from the same elevator. Jeffrey had called her ten minutes earlier, so she knew exactly where to find him.

"Where have you been?" she asked, more than a little perturbed. "Ruppert asked about the meeting with Burrelle, and I didn't know what to say."

Instead of replying, Jeffrey led her out of the building. From the look on his face, she knew this wasn't going to be good.

At the same time, the phone on Whitney's desk rang. Sitting on the sofa across the room, she held one of several placards with the As

Long As I Have Lips…I'll Have Lipstick slogan printed in various fonts and designs. From the look on her face it was apparent she wasn't happy.

The phone rang again.

She ignored it.

When it rang a third time, in a stereotypical New York City accent and attitude, Whitney yelled, "*Adam!* For Christ-sake, get that, will ya!"

The phone rang again.

"*Adam!* Where the fuck *are* you?"

She looked at her Piaget watch and realized her assistant had gone to lunch. Flinging the placard onto the floor, Whitney walked to her desk.

The phone rang again.

She picked it up and answered without the accent and attitude. She was now all business.

"Whitney Quinn's office."

"Good afternoon, Miss Quinn."

Her face drained of what little enjoyment was in her up to that point. Whitney plopped into her chair upon recognizing the voice of Dorsett & Mathers' CEO, James Dorsett.

She didn't respond, so he continued.

"After all the messages I left yesterday, it seems you forgot who I am. You *do* remember me, don't you, Sugar? My name is on your business card. It's on the wall when you walk into work. It's on your paycheck. It's even on your--"

Not wanting to hear what her boss was going to say, she interrupted with, "*Yes*, Mr. Dorsett. I remember you."

Somewhat humorously and somewhat seriously, he asked, "How much will it take for you to go back to your real last name? You know how I feel about '*Quinn.*"

Responding in the same fashion, Whitney said, "That's just *one* of the reasons why I'm keeping it, Mr. Dorsett."

"And why do you call me 'Mr. Dorsett'? What happened to James? Or--"

She cut him off, "*Because.*"

This wasn't a conversation she wanted to have, but he pressed forward.

"What's the problem, Whit? At least call me James. Even your *mother* calls me James."

Trying to stay cool and holding back her anger, Whitney answered, "Not *here!* I told you...if it ever gets out, I'll *leave.* And 'James' is just *one* of the names my mother calls you."

"I'm sure," he added with a chuckle, then asked, "How *is* your mother these days?"

Whitney's answer was short.

"No idea. We haven't spoken in a while. Now...what can I do for you?"

At a luncheonette table a couple of blocks from the office building, Jeffrey and Rekha sat opposite each other. Having devoured her food, Rekha's plate was empty, so she reached across to pick at the fries next to his untouched burger and said, "So the first thing you've got to do is locate this Italian woman and find out who she said it to."

"Sure," he replied sarcastically. "How many attractive, Italian speaking brunettes can there *be* in Manhattan?" He let that sink into Rekha's head, then said, "A few thousand people *work* in that building. Another few thousand pass through it every day. How do I know she wasn't one of *them?* She could be on a gondola in Venice right now."

Slurping her soda, she answered, "Good point, white boy. This may be harder than we thought."

Amused by her choice of words, Jeffrey asked, "Rekha, where are you from?"

"Mumbai, India. I thought you would have figured that out by now."

He laughed and replied, "No, I mean here…in New York."

"The Lower East Side. Why?" she asked.

Having heard that it was a trendy-yet-tough part of the City, he answered, "I…uh, I'm just…uhm, no reason."

Seeing his hesitation and uncertainty of what to say, Rekha retorted, "You don't hang downtown much, do you?"

In the five months since Jeffrey had arrived from Montana, he had never been below 14th Street. He answered the question by shyly shaking his head.

"Look, you know one thing for sure," his assistant said firmly. "This Italian woman had contact with someone from D-and-M, and it got to Whitney Quinn. So start there. But first, tell me what you know about Whitney Quinn."

Momentarily appearing proud that he did some background work on his new adversary, Jeffrey answered, "She's thirty-three years old, VP of Dorsett and Mathers on the fifty-second floor of the Warner Center's South Tower, and--"

Rekha burst in with, "Whitney Quinn is *not* just a VP!"

Jeffrey knew he was in for a lesson, so he sat back and listened.

"Six years ago she became the youngest female Vice President of a major agency in the entire advertising industry…*ever! Time, Forbes, Ad Age* and *Inc.* called her the most aggressive and most successful player in the last thirty years." Then Rekha reached across the table, grabbed Jeffrey's uneaten burger and took a bite.

Confused, Jeffrey politely asked, "I thought people from India didn't eat beef?"

"That's bullsh--" Once again she remembered who she was with, then corrected herself. "Are you kidding? I love a good burger or steak once-in-a-while. Besides…" with his burger in one hand, she waved her other hand around and said, "…does this look like India?"

He couldn't help but laugh as Rekha got back to business.

"Look, Jeff…Whitney Quinn came out of college and jumped into this business as if she had advertising in her veins instead of blood. She took to it like Marley took to ganja."

Unsure of what that meant, he asked, "Like *who?* To *what?*"

Shaking her head, Rekha replied, "Never mind. Forget I said it," then moved the conversation along. "All you've got to know is that if there's an account out there that Whitney Quinn wants… fugedabowdit. Just fugedabowdit." Realizing he had never seen The Sopranos or a Scorsese movie, she gave it to him in plain English. "Forget about it."

Mustering whatever bravado he had left, Jeffrey told Rekha, "Yeah, well…I'll have a meeting with this Miss Quinn to set the record straight. Where I come from, that's what we do. She may have *heard* the slogan from this Italian woman, but she'll certainly concede that it was *my* idea, and that I should be allowed to close the Divine account. After all…it's the truth."

If Jeffrey wasn't her boss, Rekha would have smacked his head to knock some sense into it. She exploded, while keeping her voice just low enough so only the surrounding tables would hear…whether they wanted to or not.

"The *truth?* In *this* city? In *this* business? In *any* business? You *do* know where you are, right? You wanna play here? Then you gotta be more aggressive and more cutthroat than the competition. Plain and simple. And in this case, your competition is Whitney-fuckin'-Quinn."

His eyes rose at her language, but he let her keep talking…not that he would have been able to stop her.

Rekha tried to calm herself as she continued, "Look, Mr. Holland…*Jeff*…you know I think you're a good-guy-and-stuff, so here's a news-flash…the advertising game they play in Montana is a lot different than the one they play in New York City. And lemme tell you something…before you're halfway through your little *'Where I Come From'* speech, Whitney Quinn will eat you up, spit you out… and greenie, after she gets done with you, you won't be able to get a job selling ad space in New Jersey." Then she finished by taking another bite of his burger.

Confusion encompassed his face as he embarrassingly asked, "Greenie?"

As she chewed, she blurted out, "*Jeez*, far-from-homeboy! A *'greenie'*…it's someone who's not ripe yet. You know…the *'new guy.'*" Then, shaking her head, she said in a combination of Yiddish, English and Hindi, "*Oy!* American people kaise itni door tak pahonchte hay? Yeh main kaghi samaz nahi paunga," which meant, "*Oy!* How these Americans got as far as they did, I'll never know."

Realizing it would be best not to know the translation, Jeffrey suggested, "How about if I offer to take her to dinner? I know she's a little older than me, but I'm a man, she's a woman. I may be able to appeal to her--"

As Rekha returned what was left of the burger to his plate, she interrupted to advise him, "*Don't even go there.* You wanna talk about getting eaten up and spit out? Don't *go there.*"

He shrugged and asked, "Why?"

Rekha leaned back in her chair, crossed her arms and shook her head…but didn't respond. Her actions spoke volumes.

Just then the waitress dropped the check in front of Jeffrey, causing him to grasp that this was the second uneaten meal he was paying for that day, and both times he had been educated in the underbelly of the advertising world by women who certainly knew more about how business was done in *the City* than he did.

CHAPTER 6
"What Are You, Crazy…*Or Stupid?*"

The constant smell of cigarette smoke permeated through the closed door adorned with a brass plate reading, "Wayne McCoslin – Director of Personnel." Most of the Dorsett & Mathers employees who needed to pass the portal did so as fast and as far to the other side of the hallway as possible.

Some did it because they didn't like the odor.

The majority did it because they didn't like the man inside.

Sitting in his 52nd floor office, Wayne McCoslin was in his late fifties, but anyone passing him on the street would say he was easily two decades older.

His desk phone rang twice before he put his half-smoked cigarette in the ashtray resting next to a framed photograph of his nineteen-year old daughter, then raised the receiver. The only reason he took the call was because it came through on his private office line.

"McCoslin," he gruffly said.

"Good afternoon, Wayne. James Dorsett here."

The fact that it was the company's CEO didn't give McCoslin any concern. To him, it was just another of Dorsett's calls that would give McCoslin a reason to do work he couldn't delegate to a subordinate.

"What can I do for you, Mr. Dorsett?" he asked, matter-of-factly.

"Wayne, I need to make a couple of personnel changes, and I want it taken care of right away. So write this down."

With his usual irritated facial expression, McCoslin made the "jerk off" motion with his free hand as he reached into a drawer to grab a pencil. Putting it to a pad, he grudgingly said, "Go ahead."

"Pablo Arenas," came from Dorsett.

The mention of the name caused McCoslin to press on the pencil, resulting in the point snapping and him asking in a surprised and louder than normal tone, "*Who?*"

His boss answered, "Pablo Arenas. I hear he was *putting in* some overtime this weekend. Good man. We notice things like that. Someone like that needs to be recognized by management. Don't you agree, Wayne?"

McCoslin grabbed another pencil, put it to the pad and, holding back his anger, asked, "What would you like me to do with him, Mr. Dorsett?"

The CEO got right to it.

"Effective immediately…I'm naming him Assistant Director of Personnel."

Dorsett heard the snap of another pencil's point.

"Mr. Dorsett, he's *a janitor!*" McCoslin barked…to the wrong person.

"Wayne…you of *all* people should know '*custodian*' is the correct job title."

With the cigarette now in his hand and up to his lips, McCoslin inhaled, then exhaled as he asked, "Mr. Dorsett, do you really think--"

"Yes I do, and I said 'effective immediately.'"

Defeated, McCoslin took another deep drag, then exhaled and sourly answered, "Yes, sir. Is there anything else?" hoping the call would be over.

"I'm glad you asked. Are you writing this down?"

McCoslin put yet another pencil to the pad and prepared himself.

"Yes, sir."

Dorsett's response was rapid.

"Process his promotion as soon as we hang up. Also, you shouldn't let *anyone* use your code-key…so clear out your stuff. You're fired."

Stunned, McCoslin snapped the pencil in half as his eyes went to his daughter's framed photograph.

The office door opened and the two earpiece-wearing Security Guards walked directly to the desk. One of them held a cardboard box.

Shocked at the entrance of the unannounced corporate hitmen, McCoslin dropped the receiver. The other guard picked it up and returned it to McCoslin's ear so he could hear Dorsett say, "Now kill that cigarette, process Pablo's paperwork…and get out."

The Security Guard hung up the phone, then they stood on each side of the desk looking down at McCoslin and watched as he promoted the custodian, the same one caught having sex with the soon-to-be-former executive's daughter on the very desk he was sitting behind, to Assistant Director of Personnel.

Down on the 44th floor, a *very* sullen Jeffrey sat behind his desk and watched as the iPad's screen turned white.

The lower section of an Asian woman's face with her lips covered in blue lipstick was in the center. In the lower right corner the words *Mood Indigo…by Divine* appeared.

The model sensuously said in Japanese, "Kuchibiru ga arukagiri… Kuchibeni o tsukeruwa."

In the lower left corner, *Lips by Izumi* appeared as the screen faded to black.

Just as he hung his head in disappointment, the desk phone rang.

He tapped the button for the speakerphone to hear Rekha say, "Ruppert's on the line. Are you out?"

Not wanting to hide the truth from his boss, Jeffrey took a deep breath, and with resolve in his voice, said, "No. Send it through."

Once Rekha clicked off, the junior executive looked at the framed photograph on his desk and sorrowfully said, "This isn't going to be good, Mom."

The phone rang.

He put on the bravest face he had and answered, "Yes, sir?"

Less than ten minutes later, Jeffrey was standing in front of the large oak desk belonging to David Ruppert, one of AOR's partners. Specifically, the R.

One side wall was covered in Clio awards, each with a poster corresponding to that particular product's campaign. The opposite wall housed more than a dozen silent TV monitors, allowing Ruppert to observe which major networks were advertising what products and when they were being aired.

David Ruppert wasn't sitting at his desk. He was standing behind it with his back facing Jeffrey, allowing the mid-seventies executive to look down 8th Avenue as he angrily grilled and yelled at his nervous, young employee.

"*You used the same slogan Whitney Quinn used?*" Before Jeffrey had the chance to answer, Ruppert continued barking, "What are you, crazy...*or stupid?*"

Jeffrey could see from the veins in Ruppert's forehead that the tongue-lashing was far from over.

"Holland...you've opened this company up to a probable lawsuit and scandal that could put us out of business!"

Jeffery tried to get in, "She got the slogan from--"

But Ruppert continued ranting.

"I *knew* I should have given it to someone with experience and not let a greenie like you run with it! But I liked your concept, I liked your idea for the presentation...so I gave you a shot. Now I'm going to catch a world of shit for it! Do you know what it cost to put that presentation together in time for your meeting? And god-fucking-damn it, *you said the slogan was your idea!*"

Jeffrey had to state his case, whether his boss wanted to hear it or not.

"It *was* my idea!"

"Then how did Quinn get it?" Ruppert countered.

Due to his nervousness, Jeffrey's answers came out in short sentences.

"Yesterday. In the elevator. This woman was putting on lipstick."

Having no alternative but to hear it, Ruppert asked, "Is this a long story?"

Jeffrey nodded, so Ruppert sat and eased into the high-back leather chair behind his desk. He motioned to the chair Jeffrey was standing next to and said, "Then sit down, start from the beginning, and just remember…your fucking job is on the line."

Visibly sweating, Jeffery sat facing his boss and his future…and began his story.

Though it took less than three minutes for Jeffrey to get to the end of his chronicle, his hands and brow were wet as he leaned toward Ruppert.

"…so I walked out, got on the next elevator and had the Art Department working on that exact slogan five minutes after I said it. Then I put it in front of the focus group. The results, along with the storyboards and slogan, were in your hands by four-forty. Thirty minutes later I was filming models in the studio." Then Jeffrey innocently shook his head, sat back into the chair and said, "I don't get it. Where I come from…it would be as simple as speaking to her--"

"Do you really think I care about how business was done back on the farm, Holland?"

Jeffrey was shocked at the lack of understanding and compassion as Ruppert continued his verbal assault.

"Now get your ass back on that elevator…go up to the fifty-second floor…get in front of Whitney Quinn and tell her you solicited Divine with the same slogan she did. Then get down on your fucking knees and beg for forgiveness. Do you hear me?"

The command and question angered Jeffrey, but he held it in as Ruppert continued, "And may the Advertising Gods have mercy on you if this leaks out! Because if it does, you won't be able to get a job selling ad space…"

They simultaneously stood, each with contempt for the other, and said, "…in *New Jersey!*"

Ruppert scowled, "Now get out of my office and do whatever you've got to do to save this company…*and your job!*"

Jeffrey turned and walked toward the door…feeling Ruppert's eyes burn into his back.

"Adam," Whitney called out as she stepped from her office, "I'm done for today."

He looked at the clock on his monitor. 4:18PM.

"It's good to be the boss," he thought to himself.

The Vice President was halfway down the hall before he could say, "See you tomorrow!"

Whitney sauntered through the reception area and grabbed one of a dozen fashion magazines strategically placed on a table, then saw Wayne McCoslin between the two Security Guards, sullen, in need of a cigarette and holding his box of personal items while waiting for an elevator.

Walking up from behind and standing next to them, Whitney looked at the newly unemployed executive and dryly said, "You know, Wayne, maybe if you smiled more…"

The elevator bell chimed and the doors opened. Whitney stepped inside, turned, faced the three men and pressed the "Lobby" button. The Security Guards held McCoslin's shoulders, preventing him from boarding the elevator. He looked at Whitney as if waiting for her to finish what she was saying.

But she didn't…and the doors closed.

At the same time, a dejected Jeffrey, after his scolding and reprimand in David Ruppert's office, stood in the 44th floor's elevator bay and tapped the "Up" button. He was so distraught that he had inadvertently walked past Nora the receptionist and neglected to smile, wave or have something complimentary to say. She could tell something was wrong…and felt sorry for the young man from Montana.

While waiting, Jeffrey collected his thoughts and quietly recited to himself the speech he was going to make to the woman who had somehow stolen his slogan and was now going to be responsible for his firing and returning home…home to the farm.

"Good afternoon, Miss Quinn," he softly said, "My name is Jeffrey Holland and I work for Arthur, O'Connell and Ruppert. Earlier today I had a meeting with Gail Burrelle, and I--"

Ding!

The elevator arrived before he could continue.

The door opened and a FedEx delivery-person quickly wheeled out a small cart of boxes. It distracted Jeffrey, causing him to step onto the elevator without noticing the "Down" arrow. There were a few people inside. One of them was Whitney, whose eyes were glued to an ad in the magazine. The new occupant went unnoticed as the doors closed.

He tapped "52," but once he felt the elevator going down he realized his mistake and was quickly embarrassed, knowing *someone* must have seen him hit the now-lit button for the 52nd floor.

"Damn," he muttered. Afraid he said it too loud, he looked around and followed it with an apologetic "Sorry" to anyone he may have offended. But "damn" wasn't on *anyone's* offensive-word list... *especially* in Manhattan.

Jeffrey mentally admonished himself for the foolish error of getting on the wrong elevator, but decided to make the best of a bad situation and scan its occupants hoping to find the Italian brunette.

His eyes focused on each female face before moving to the next one, even Whitney's, but nothing clicked. Now having to kill time until he was on the 52nd floor, Jeffrey's lips silently moved as he again practiced his speech.

Upon reaching the lobby, he moved aside so everyone could walk by. Though it seemed like forever, the doors eventually closed and the elevator began to rise as Jeffrey continued to rehearse, "Good afternoon, Miss Quinn. My name is Jeffrey Holland and I work for Arthur, O'Connell and Ruppert. Earlier today I had a meeting with Gail Burrelle..."

Jeffrey sat on a comfortable chair in the reception area of Dorsett & Mathers. Tania was at her desk answering and transferring calls while Jeffrey focused on her short brunette hair, hoping to match the receptionist to the woman he had spoken to the day before.

Adam walked through the lobby and approached Jeffrey who nervously stood and shook hands.

"Hi, Mr. Holland. I'm Adam Bryant, Miss Quinn's assistant. She's left for the day, but maybe *I* can help you."

Jeffrey collected his thoughts and respectfully answered, "Thank you, but I'd like to meet with Miss Quinn as soon as possible. Can I make an appointment for the first thing in the morning? Nine o'clock?"

Knowing his boss would never arrive before ten, Adam replied, "She has an early meeting. Maybe something around eleven might work, but I'd need to check with her first. And this is for...?"

Unsure of what to say and not wanting to make his prepared speech to Adam, Jeffrey started with, "I need to discuss a presentation that…" Then he took a deep breath and cordially continued, "No offense, Mr. Bryant, but this is something I need to discuss with Miss Quinn." Jeffrey reached in his inside jacket pocket and came out with his business card. He handed it to Adam and said, "Please ask her to call me. It's *very* important."

Adam looked at the card to see AOR's logo, then equally cordial, but still in business-mode, replied, "I'll tell her. But she's *very* busy."

"I'm sure she is," Jeffrey responded. "But tell her it has to do with a new account she's working on. That's why I need to speak to her… soon. *Very* soon. Please." He knew his nervousness was evident.

So he shut up.

Hearing the importance in Jeffrey's voice, Adam pressed a little further with, "If you can give me an idea as to what it's about…"

Jeffrey politely shook his head.

Then the saddened junior executive turned and walked to the elevator bay…not knowing what would happen next.

CHAPTER 7
"You Said, 'Where *I* Come From'?"

Wednesday, May 8th was the day Jeffrey Holland would remember for the rest of his life.

Disembarking the R train and walking up the concrete steps from the 7th Avenue and West 57th Street subway station to take one of his routes to the Time Warner Center, the pep in his step wasn't there. The smile of success wasn't on his face. He showed no interest in the people passing on the street, or the buildings housing Midtown Manhattan's magnificence and history, nor the advertisements on the sides of buses.

The only thing on his mind since he left his office the day before was knowing that if he didn't connect with Whitney Quinn soon and successfully, his time in New York City's advertising industry would be limited to the next several hours.

It was exactly 9AM when Jeffrey stepped from the elevator into AOR's lobby.

In less than 48 hours he had come up with *'The Golden Slogan,'* and produced a visual campaign designed to be marketed worldwide. Then he presented it to Gail Burrelle, known as one of the most successful and respected individuals in cosmetics and advertising… and who personally praised Jeffrey for his presentation *and* talent.

Jeffrey's corporate existence now depended on Whitney Quinn, an executive from a competing company pursuing the same account. A woman he had never met nor seen thanks to her aversion of publicity and appearing in *any* media…social, print or otherwise.

Though, he rapidly became aware of her well-publicized track record of *always* getting what she went after.

Just as he had the afternoon before, he passed through AOR's lobby without smiling at Nora. And just like the day before…Nora felt sorry for the young junior executive from Montana.

Jeffrey scanned his code-key and made his way along the hallway toward his office. He did what he could to smile to a few of the assistants, but they could see his heart wasn't in it.

Several feet before Jeffrey reached Rekha's desk, David Ruppert appeared as if magically from behind and bellowed so everyone could hear, "*Holland!*"

The startled Jeffrey jumped and turned, not knowing what to say, nor what to expect.

"So?" the boss asked. "What happened yesterday?"

Jeffrey nervously responded, "She wasn't in. I'm hoping to see her today and resolve it, sir."

Ruppert made sure everyone heard him bark, "And if you don't… pack your stuff and get out!" Then he returned to his office.

All those within earshot looked sorrowfully at Jeffrey.

Rekha felt terrible for him.

Jeffrey was humiliated as he shuffled into his office and closed the door behind him.

By 9:30 he was ready to call Dorsett & Mathers. Knowing Whitney was a Vice President, it was doubtful she'd be in that early…but Jeffrey felt he had nothing to lose and wanted to get the ball rolling. With Adam's card in one hand, he dialed the desk phone with the other, then tapped the speakerphone button.

The phone rang twice before Adam answered.

"Whitney Quinn's office."

"Good morning, Adam." Jeffrey did everything he could to keep the stress in his voice under control. "This is Jeffrey Holland. I stopped in yesterday. Is there any chance Ms. Quinn is in?"

"Sorry, Mr. Holland. Ms. Quinn isn't expected until later this afternoon."

"Please…please let her know this will only take five minutes. It's really *very* important."

Adam's trained ear easily sensed the stress in the caller's voice, causing a cordial response of, "Yes sir, Mr. Holland. I will. As soon as she gets in or if she calls in for messages, I'll let her know."

"Do you need my number?"

"No, Mr. Holland…it's right here on my desk."

Adam once again asked if Jeffrey would like to provide some details, and Jeffrey once again respectfully let him know it was, "…something I'd like to discuss only with Miss Quinn."

They exchanged parting pleasantries, then hung up.

Jeffrey looked at the clock.

It just ticked to 9:32.

The digital clock on Melody Beecham' office wall read 2:54PM. Melody was Dorsett & Mathers' Art Director and had ample awards and plaques on her walls to prove she knew what she was doing. Melody stood in front of her desk with her top male and female graphic artists on each side.

Eighteen posters with designs of *the slogan* were strewn about as those in the room were being read the Riot Act…Whitney Quinn Style.

"Since yesterday morning you've been telling me you're gonna give me…" Whitney's fingers made quotation marks, "'*Exactly what Burrelle's looking for.*'" The pissed off executive pointed to the posters and kept the barrage coming. "And you give me *this shit?* What the hell am I supposed to do with *these?*"

Melody mustered the courage to ask, "Perhaps if you gave us an idea of what--?"

Whitney stopped her dead with, "*I* have to tell *you?* It's my job to *get* the account…not design the fucking artwork!" She tried to calm down, but it wasn't easy. "Look, Melody…Burrelle loves my slogan, but she wasn't impressed with your graphics. I can't make it any simpler than that. The three of you have created five of this company's best campaigns in the last three years…"

Whitney wasn't done yet…she was delaying her words for effect, then she'd make her point and leave. The artists could see the determination in her eyes and body language as she picked up her purse and stared at each of them as she said, "…but I want this account. I want this account more than any of you can comprehend or understand. I want the Divine Cosmetics account…and your jobs are on the line if Dorsett and Mathers doesn't get it. Do you hear me?"

There was nothing the three of them could say other than respectfully reply in unison, "Yes, Miss Quinn."

Then she hit them with the capper.

"And I want it by six tonight."

That was when Melody had to step forward. She pointed to the clock and defensively exclaimed, "That's in *three hours!*"

"Yes, it is," Whitney sarcastically retorted. "So why the fuck are you wasting time talking to me when you should be coming up with something?" Then she walked out the door.

Under Melody's breath, the two artists heard her say, "*Bitch.*"

They nodded their heads at the statement, then, visibly worried, looked at one another.

Adam sat at his desk typing the daily reports into his computer as a *very* pissed off Whitney returned from the Art Department. It was the first time they had seen each other all day.

He looked up and cheerfully asked, "Hello, boss! Having a good day?"

"Not now. I'm not in the fuckin' mood. Get me an eight o'clock dinner with Gail Burrelle."

Adam's head returned to the computer monitor, knowing it was best to avoid any conversation when she was in such a state of mind.

"I'll let you know when it's confirmed," he assured her.

Just before Whitney continued to her office, she asked, "Any calls?"

Adam nodded his head but didn't look up or stop typing. She walked over as his hand instinctively went to a small pile of messages on his desk, raised his arm and handed them to his boss. Jeffrey Holland's was on top.

Eyeing it, she read, "'Needs to speak about your new account.'" She asked in rapid succession, "What's *that* mean? *Which* new account? Who is Jeffrey Holland?"

Finally looking up, her assistant efficiently answered, "The Account Exec for AOR. He came up yesterday after you left. You got an email about it last night *and* this morning. So far, he's called three times today."

Whitney asked, "What *about* my 'new account'?"

"He wouldn't say," Adam replied as he looked under a sheet of paper to find Jeffrey's card. Handing it to her, he continued, "Whatever it is, he says it's '*very* important,' and needs to speak to you right away."

Having only the Divine account on her mind, Whitney showed her disinterest in whatever Jeffrey Holland wanted to discuss.

"I'm going into my office," she said without her normal enthusiasm. "I need a drink."

Once she turned to leave, Adam thought he should tell her something else.

"Oh…Mr. Dorsett called. He *also* said it's '*very* important,' and needs to speak to you right away, and to call him at the--"

Whitney jumped in with, "At the beach house."

Adam triumphally responded with, "At the townhouse on Riverside Drive."

She stopped just before opening one of the double-doors, then slowly and quietly asked, "He's in the City?"

"Looks that way," Adam answered, then returned to work.

Whitney walked into her sanctuary, closed the door, took two steps inside and under her breath said, "*Shit.*"

The sadness on Jeffrey Holland's face was beyond description as he looked at the clock for the eighty-seventh time in the last few hours. This time it read 3:33.

He placed his two awards in an empty packing box that sat atop the desk and slid his iPad into the soft leather briefcase.

The phone rang. Jeffrey's breathing stopped for a second or two, He was certain that Ruppert was calling to fire him.

By the third ring he summoned the courage and raised the receiver.

"Yes?"

An uneasiness ran through him when he heard Rekha's words, "It's *her*...on two."

Jeffrey took a deep breath and gently tapped the speakerphone button. He did whatever he could to be cool and professional as he spoke.

"Good afternoon, Miss Quinn. Thank you for returning my call."

"Mr. Holland, you left a message...something about my 'new account'"?

He closed his eyes and mouthed the beginning of his memorized speech.

Whitney sat at her desk awaiting a response over *her* speakerphone as she held up his business card. She briefly considered refilling the shot glass in front of her from the bottle of tequila next to the phone. Then...

"On Monday, around noon, there was a woman...an attractive woman who spoke Italian. She dropped her lipstick in the elevator. I picked it up and said, 'As long as women have lips...they'll have lipstick.'"

Whitney was astonished to realize he was the '*man with manners*' in the elevator.

"Well, the next thing I know..." he paused to think of the right way to say what needed to be said.

Whitney pressed him.

"Yes?"

Jeffrey gathered his courage and continued.

"Yesterday morning I...I apparently used the same slogan you did in my presentation to Gail Burrelle."

Whitney's anger was instant as it came through the speaker.

"You *what?* To *who?*"

He continued, "She said you had presented the same slogan to her the night before."

Unknown to Jeffrey and Whitney, Rekha was listening on her phone...making sure she had hit the Mute button so no one could hear her breathing.

In an arrogant New York City attitude, Whitney shot back with, "I'm not sure if I like where this call is headed, Mr. Holland. Get to the point."

"I don't want to get off on the wrong foot, Miss Quinn, but..." Jeffrey paused for a deep breath to help him remain professional and courteous, then continued, "...I originated that slogan in the elevator. It was certainly presented to you through a second party who heard it from me. Based on that alone, I should be allowed to use it."

Whitney held back her laughter, and asked, "You're kidding, right?"

Her response dumbfounded him and brought out his nervousness. He was searching for something to say...so he did.

"Well, no...I'm *not* kidding, and I'd like to meet with you, personally...to discuss this like professionals. That's how we settle things...where I come from."

Hearing Jeffrey's words caused Rekha to involuntarily smack herself in the head...and grateful she had hit the Mute button.

Whitney responded, "Look..." eyeing his name on the card as she spoke, "Jeffrey, I'm very busy. I really don't think we have a reason to get together, and I *certainly* wouldn't discuss a potential account with someone from another company. I'm sure even where *you* come from...they understand that."

Her last remark infuriated the junior executive, so he shot back.

"Where *I* come from, Miss Quinn, we do business the way it's supposed to be done, legitimately, professionally and honestly... without wrongfully using another person's idea."

Inquisitively, the Vice President asked, "Where *are* you from, Mr. Holland?"

Jeffrey *and* Rekha swallowed hard as he replied, "Pine Creek, Montana."

Whitney rolled her eyes and shook her head, while the others on the call heard her exhale and utter, "*Oy.*"

Jeffrey wasn't up on his Yiddish, so he asked, "Excuse me?"

Whitney wanted to end the conversation.

"Okay listen, I have to go. So, let me give you some advice." The sarcasm in her voice became evident. "If you don't know how to play in the big city, then go back to whatever little farm-town you came from...and get plowed." Then she hit the speakerphone button and disconnected the call.

A dial-tone blared through Jeffrey's speaker. His hand came down on the button with a force he had never experienced before. He stared at the phone...not knowing what to do or say next.

That was when Rekha angrily stuck her head in the door and growled, "'*Where I come from*'? You said, '*Where I come from*'?"

Without raising his eyes from the phone, he commanded as he had never done before, "Get her back on the line, Raye."

His assistant retreated and closed the door as Jeffrey sat back... plotting.

That was when the door reopened. This time it was a visibly unhappy David Ruppert who entered. He approached the desk before Jeffrey had a chance to react or greet him. Looking at the packing box, Ruppert's snarled and asked, "Talk to Quinn?"

"Yes, sir."

"Is it resolved?"

"Not yet, but I'm hoping--"

"Then that's it," Ruppert interrupted. "Turn in your code-key and get out. And Holland...you'd better hope she doesn't sue us! 'Cause if she does, I'll personally go to Wyoming, find you and drag your ass back to take the fall."

Jeffrey had no interest in correcting Ruppert's error about his home state.

The desk phone rang. Jeffrey looked at it with hope in his eyes.

"Forget it!" the boss barked. "No more calls! You don't work here anymore! And take everything that has to do with that stupid, unoriginal presentation and--"

The door opened and Rekha stuck her head in.

"Excuse me, Mr. Holland...it's your call with--"

Ruppert turned and yelled at her, "He's not taking any more calls! Now get out!"

"But sir, it's--"

The veins in Ruppert's head bulged and his volume increased.

"I said *no more calls!* Or maybe you'd like to join this idiot in his job search?"

Rekha no longer cared what Ruppert had to say. Her attention turned to the dejected Jeffrey, who could only shrug and motion his head for her to get out and save her job.

Once again, his assistant retreated and closed the door.

Ruppert returned his attention to the focus of his fury, and asked, "Where the fuck was I?"

Realizing he was already fired and had nothing to lose, Jeffrey imitated Ruppert's bark and answered, "*And take everything that has to do with that stupid, unoriginal presentation and…*'"

The imitation pissed Ruppert off even more, but that didn't stop him from continuing the salvo.

"…and get it out of this office! As far as this company's concerned, we had *nothing* to do with it. If Quinn's lawyers come knocking, I'm gonna tell them it was all *your* idea, and that *you* own it!"

Once again, no longer caring what he said that would offend his now former-boss, Jeffrey overconfidently egged him on by asking, "Care to put that in writing?"

Ruppert looked down at the young, now-*former*-junior executive and bellowed, "My pleasure, smartass! That will help us document who's *fully responsible* for this mess." He turned and walked to the door as he continued, "It'll be ready for your signature before you leave!" then stormed out…leaving the door open behind him.

It took a while for Jeffrey to absorb what had just happened before he sadly stood and carefully put more items in the packing box. Near tears, he picked up the photograph of he and his mother from his desk.

"Looks like I'll be coming back a lot sooner than I thought, Mom."

He didn't see Rekha watching him, nor did he see the tears welling in her eyes as he carefully placed the photograph in the box.

Adam had his phone's receiver to his ear as Whitney emerged from her office and walked toward him. Seeing that he wasn't in the midst of a conversation, she said, "I just spoke with that Holland guy."

Adam pointed to the phone and told her, "I was just about to call you. I have his assistant on hold…he wants to talk to you again."

"Forget it," was her response. "He said he used the same--"

"Miss Quinn?" came from an unknown voice down the hallway.

It was Pablo Arenas, the mid-twenties custodian partly responsible for Wayne McCoslin's firing the day before. Pablo, uncomfortably dressed in a suit with a poorly knotted tie, was approaching Whitney and Adam.

They looked at him, confused.

When he was just a few feet away he asked again, "Miss Quinn?"

"Yes?"

As he started to speak, his Hispanic accent became readily apparent.

"Miss Quinn, mi llamo es Pablo Arenas. I am the new…" Finding it difficult to pronounce the words, he spoke slowly to make sure he got them right. "…Assistant Directore' of the Personnel. Actually, they say I am the Directore' until Mr. Dorsett, you padre, you father, he find someone to--"

Adam and Whitney, both shocked, but for different reasons, loudly asked in unison, "*Who?*"

Pablo innocently replied, "Mr. Dorsett…you father."

Whitney and Adam looked at one another…each were stunned. Whitney, speechless, leaned against the wall, refusing to hear what was just said.

Adam dropped the phone onto his desk…dumfounded, not knowing what to ask or say.

That didn't stop Pablo.

"He take me to lunch. Very nice man. Muy simpático. I think he may have drank more than he should have, but very nice man. Muy simpático. He say I owe my job to you. I don't know what I did to deserve it, but…I want to tell you I appreciate la oportunidad…the op…por…tunity you give me. Muchas gracias." He put his hand out to shake. She weakly extended hers. As they shook hands, Pablo respectfully again said, "Muchas gracias," then turned and walked toward his office…the one where he was caught having sex with his girlfriend, Wayne McCoslin's daughter.

Without saying a word to Adam, Whitney turned, entered her office and slammed the door. Adam was still so stunned and confused by what had just happened that he didn't hear Rekha's voice coming through the receiver.

"Hello? Hell-ooo? Oh well."

Click. She hung up.

In the Art Department, Melody Beecham and her two graphic artists were mulling over new examples of artwork for *the slogan*. There were a few designs she felt good about, but more than anything she was proud of what they had quickly achieved as she looked at the wall clock. It was only 4:02.

That was when the phone on her desk rang.

"Art Director," Melody answered. She listened for a few seconds before saying, "But Miss Quinn, we think we have two or three great--"

She stopped.

The line went dead.

Extremely confused, Melody turned to her talented subordinates and explained, "She said, 'Cancel the Divine project'…and hung up."

They humbly looked at their new *As Long As I Have Lips* posters… and realized it was just another day in the advertising business.

Then, at the same time, they each said, "*Son-of-a-bitch.*"

CHAPTER 8
"I...Am...Whitney Quinn"

Tears filled Nora's eyes as she watched Jeffrey stand at the elevator bay with his leather briefcase slung over his right shoulder and both hands holding an overstuffed box of possessions. He was still in a stupor from the last hour that resulted in the demise of his dream.

This time when the elevator doors parted he looked at the directional arrow to make sure this one was going down, "Just like my career," he thought as he stepped aboard the same elevator where he had encountered the Italian beauty. It only took a second to notice the woman standing against the back wall using both hands to hold *two* boxes, with the top one covering her face.

He turned to the closing doors to see the Lobby button was already lit.

Once the elevator began its decent, Jeffrey, though filled with pent-up anxiety and anger, maintained his manners and said, "I'm sorry, ma'am. If my hands weren't full, I'd take those for you. If you'd like, we can slide that top one on mine."

Whitney, the woman holding the boxes, thought the man's voice sounded vaguely familiar, so, poking her head out from the side, she said, "That's very nice. I'm okay...thanks."

Jeffrey turned, causing them to smile at one another, but because of his state of despair, he wasn't paying attention enough to recall ever hearing *her* voice.

Doing a doubletake, Whitney recognized the man who had gallantly picked up her lipstick. She immediately knew to maintain a level of calm. Of course, calmness came easy once she remembered that he had never met Whitney Quinn…just an Italian-speaking brunette who wore dark sunglasses and a hat.

Eyeing her boxes, Jeffrey asked, "Did you get canned?"

Cautiously, she responded, "No. I went voluntarily. What about you?"

The question brought his confusion and frustration of what happened to the surface, releasing emotions that caused him to ramble, "I'm not really sure! I did everything right. I even got my boss's approval. I don't get it. I mean, where I come from…"

Whitney's eyes went wide at hearing those words and retreated behind the boxes so Jeffrey couldn't see her reaction.

"…when people have a discrepancy, they should sit down to talk things over, right? They work it out," then uttered, "I told my boss the truth, but he didn't want to hear it." Jeffrey lowered his head and confessed, "I even called the woman who stole my idea…"

Whitney again inched her head out ever-so-slightly and asked, "You lost your job over that?"

Jeffrey grimly replied, "Yeah," then raised his head, did a doubletake of his own and probed, "Huh? What? Over *what?* Someone stealing my idea?" He again hung his head and, as if ashamed to speak, softly answered, "Yes."

Whitney lowered her boxes a bit and studied Jeffrey, thinking, "This guy lost his job because of me, and he has no idea who I am." But when she spoke, it came out as, "How about we go for a drink?"

Taken aback, he asked, "Excuse me?"

She gave her tried-and-true smile, the one that always worked to divert a man's attention. She wanted to keep Jeffrey from thinking about her reference to his being fired, nor did she want him to ask who she was…yet.

"A drink. C'mon…we *both* had a shitty day. My treat."

Having never been asked to have a drink by a woman in New York *or* Montana, Jeffrey wasn't sure how to react or reply, so he unsuccessfully tried to stall.

"It's a little early for a drink, isn't it?"

For the second time that day, though Jeffrey didn't know it, Whitney had to hold back laughing at his naivete.

"Early? It's a after four-thirty!"

"I'm sorry," he said, hoping to find another excuse. He raised the box and offered, "I've got *this*, and I've got to get a cab."

Getting Jeffrey to go for a drink was now Whitney's goal.

"Neither's a problem," she declared with a sly bird-of-prey grin.

The younger man had no comeback.

Other than Rekha, Jeffrey had never been confronted by an assertive woman like the one he was sharing the elevator with.

Ding! They arrived at their destination and the doors parted. Ever the gentleman, Jeffrey stepped aside, allowing Whitney to exit first.

Strutting past him, she commanded, "Let's go!"

Unsure of what to say, he obediently followed the woman peering over her boxes and walking toward the 58th Street doors to her waiting chauffeur.

Jeffrey watched Stuart race to Whitney and take the boxes. With his arms full, Stuart used his back to push the door open for his boss and the box-carrying person following her.

Whitney told the driver, "He's with me." Stuart nodded and led the two newly unemployed executives through the late-afternoon flow of pedestrians to the white limo parked at the curb.

With Jeffrey several feet behind, Whitney whispered to Stuart not to address her by name in front of her new friend. Knowing his boss for years, there was no need to reply…just a quick nod of his head.

Resting Whitney's boxes on the fender, Stuart popped the trunk with the key fob and placed them inside. Then he walked to the still stupefied Jeffrey and took his box and briefcase. Just before the trunk was closed, Jeffrey instinctively reached in and retrieved the briefcase. He didn't know why…but he felt the iPad was the only thing holding what was left of his life and failed career, and he wanted it close.

Stuart opened the rear passenger door, awaiting his orders, causing Whitney to ask Jeffrey, "Where would you like to go?"

Unsure of what to say and out of his comfort zone, he could only shrug. The usually clear-headed ex-junior executive had no idea where to go…*especially* for a drink.

Since arriving in New York, Jeffrey had lived as he promised himself and his mother. Drinking, fast-talking women and indulging in an extravagant lifestyle were just three of the things he swore to avoid.

Yet, here he was with this fast-talking woman with a limousine… going for a drink.

He didn't know *what* to think. But somehow his brain justified the situation with, "The dream is over. It doesn't matter what I do tonight because unless I want to sell ad space in New Jersey and be known as '*The man who stole Whitney Quinn's Divine campaign,*' I'll be going back to Montana as soon as I pack my bags."

Still waiting for a response, Whitney couldn't hold back the laughter and asked, "Do I have to handle this?"

Even Stuart turned away so his chuckle wasn't seen.

Whitney was exactly where she wanted to be…in the position of control. She cooed to Jeffrey, "Please get in and join me," and then gave Stuart his orders, "I want a view *of* the City, not be *in* it."

"Yes, ma'am," came from both men.

Mesmerized by what was being offered, Jeffrey slid onto the backseat as if being drawn by a magnet.

Once the limo started moving, Whitney made sure the conversation concerned nothing too important, and did whatever possible to distract him from asking the wrong questions…such as about herself or the advertising industry.

They exited the Lincoln Tunnel less than 12 minutes later.

Seeing the "Welcome To New Jersey" sign for the first time, Jeffrey asked, "Taking me where I can get a job selling ad space?" Not knowing what his question meant, Whitney was at a loss for an answer.

Less than five minutes later the limo cruised along Weehawken's Lincoln Harbor Pier and stopped in front of The Chart House. Valets rushed to the rear passenger doors and opened them for the occupants as they exited in mid-conversation.

"But you still haven't told me which company you worked for," said Jeffrey, with his ever-present briefcase over his shoulder and not paying attention to the surroundings.

Heading toward the restaurant's entrance, Whitney responded, "It's been a bitch of a day, Jeffrey, and I need a drink first." Then she seductively questioned, "You know, I never asked before I kidnapped you, but…do you need to be home? Is there a *Mrs.* Holland waiting somewhere?"

The question took him by surprise. Somewhat flattered, he answered, "No. I'm not married. I--" He suddenly rethought what she said, stopped their forward motion and retorted, "Wait a minute! How did you know my name? We never introduced ourselves!"

Thinking quickly, Whitney gave an enticing grin and answered, "*You* told me, silly."

He returned with a very definite, "I did not."

"Yes you did. Between Ninth and Tenth Avenue."

Jeffrey paused to think about it. Whitney knew she would win this one.

"Are you sure?" he asked.

She won.

With a grin on her beautiful face, Whitney grabbed his arm and led him to the door, confidently saying, "Your name's Jeffrey Holland, you grew up in Montana and worked for Arthur, O'Connell & Ruppert…if I remember correctly."

Jeffrey concentrated as hard as he could but came up blank as he stuttered, "And you're…you're…"

Leaning toward him as if waiting to hear her name…Whitney pouted ever so adorably.

Confused and feeling guilty, he continued, "I'm sorry. I really am. With everything that's happened…my presentation, getting fired, the limo, New Jersey…my head's pretty fuzzy. Please, tell me again. I won't forget."

She responded with, "C'mon, let's have that drink first."

Jeffrey, being Jeffrey, reached for the door and opened it, which, like the rest of his gentlemanly ways, didn't go unnoticed by Whitney. Just as when she was the dark-haired Italian who dropped her tube of lipstick, and as the stranger carrying two boxes, she was taken by his manners and chivalry.

He watched her elegantly glide past him. For the first time he saw how stunning she really was.

Within a moment they were escorted to a table against the window with the Hudson River a dozen yards away and the magnificent view of Manhattan's skyline…from the Battery and Freedom Tower on the south end, to the George Washington Bridge to the north. The sun in the western sky reflected off the steel and glass skyscrapers. It was unlike anything Jeffrey had ever seen. His astonishment was only equaled by Whitney's as she watched this innocent younger man take it all in.

He also found it hard to grasp that 30 minutes earlier he had conversed with this unknown woman and now they were watching cruise ships and ferries maneuver up, down and across the waterway.

As he had put the strap of his briefcase over the back of his chair, their waitress stepped up to the table, introduced herself with a smile, told the couple she hoped they were having a nice evening and asked what each would like to drink.

Though the waitress first looked to Jeffrey, ever the gentleman, he made sure Whitney ordered first…and she certainly knew what she wanted as she rattled off, "A Ketel One Dickens Martini, *up*."

"For you, sir?"

Dazed by Whitney's quick order and unsure of what it was, Jeffrey spoke the only words he knew for such a situation, "A beer, please."

"Tap or bottle? Domestic or imported? A local micro-brewery?"

Seeing Jeffrey's confusion, Whitney jumped in with, "A Corona with lime."

Once the waitress walked away, Jeffrey's look of appreciation was evident, then he asked, "A Dickens Martini?"

Grinning at his innocence, she leaned and told him, "I never like anything in my martinis, so a Dickens has no olive or twist in it. *Get it?* No olive or twist? '*Oliver Twist*'? *Dickens?*"

By the look on his face she realized he *didn't* get it…especially when he confessed, "I wouldn't know. I've never had a martini."

Leaning back into the cushioned chair, Whitney's eyes sparkled as she continued to find him adorable.

She flirtatiously quipped, "Well, maybe we'll have to have one or two someday."

Again at a loss for the right thing to say, Jeffrey respectfully smiled, then returned his stare to the low sun's reflection off the skyline.

Fifteen minutes later Whitney's martini glass had a sip or two remaining. With only a sip or two taken, Jeffrey's beer was practically full because he had been doing most of the talking, and she was engrossed in his words.

"Actually, I grew up on a two-hundred-acre farm in Pine Creek with about eighty head of cattle, a few horses and crops of wheat and barley. I got my BA at Montana State University, then worked for a pretty big agency…well, big for Montana." His red-blooded All-American pride beamed as he finished with, "A couple of my campaigns even won awards."

Whitney grinned and tried to sound impressed. "Oh really?" she asked, recalling her office wall was covered with them. "Clios?"

Jeffrey's face turned humble as he answered, "No." He took a deep breath and a sip of beer before continuing with, "But for Montana they were the best a rep could get."

Whitney prodded to find out more with, "Are they what got you the job in the City?"

"Somehow Mr. Ruppert had heard about me. I had an interview on Skype, and they made me an offer better than *anything* I would've gotten back home. So I came to New York a little over five months ago and started--"

"Five months?" she asked, quite astonished. "That's all you've been here?"

He hung his head, embarrassed by the short time of his brief rise to success…and his rapid fall to being unemployed. He didn't notice the look on the woman's face across from him that showed she was captivated by his innocence.

His head still down and looking at the Corona, he said, "I was on my way to landing what could've been one of the biggest accounts of my life when this woman…this Whitney Quinn…stole my slogan." This time he took a mouthful of beer, swallowed and let the alcohol do the talking, "I'll show *her* I know how to '*play in the big city*,' damn it!"

Whitney's air of innocence never faltered as Jeffrey gave a boyish look and said, "I'm sorry. I didn't mean to lose my temper like that."

Before Whitney could comprehend why he was apologizing, Jeffrey stood and said, "It's been one heck of a day. Would you excuse me? I'd like to find the Men's Room."

Whitney politely nodded and watched him walk away with a look of, "Is this guy *real?*" on her face.

As Jeffrey approached the hostess for directions to the rest room, Whitney reached into her purse, grabbed her cell phone, hit a programmed number and put it to her ear.

Adam was sitting with friends and drinking martinis in one of Manhattan's trendy bars. Feeling his cell phone buzz within his suit jacket, he reached in and looked at the Caller ID. There was no hesitation in answering it.

"Where are you? Are you all right?" he quickly asked.

"I'm fine and I'm in New Jersey."

Relief and confusion were in his responses of, "Good…and *Jersey?*"

"Don't ask, but I--"

"Will you be in tomorrow?" Adam interrupted.

"No. I quit. You know that."

His expression went to sadness as he tried to talk her out of it.

"I *quit!* I FedEx'd my resignation. He'll get it tomorrow. I'm out," Whitney snapped while watching for Jeffrey's return.

"Is he really your--"

"Yes, Adam…he's really my father," She said with more than a little anger in her eyes, voice and body language. She turned serious and continued, "Listen…I need you to do some digging. Get a pen."

Adam reached into his inside pocket, pulled out his Mont Blanc Classique, moved his martini and put the tip to the paper napkin… ready to take orders from his boss as he always did, even though she wasn't his boss anymore.

Jeffrey approached the table. Whitney knocked back the last of her martini and raised the empty glass as the waitress walked by, then the beautiful advertising executive turned to admire the view. Without her seeing him look, he was again taken by a beauty he had never seen before.

Reaching his seat, Whitney seductively eyed him and began talking before he had a chance to say anything.

"I'll tell you something, Jeffrey…any company foolish enough to lose a guy like you, well, they must be run by idiots."

Appreciating the compliment, he humbly smiled, then raised his glass of beer and tilted it to her. After taking a mouthful, he replied, "I can say the same about whoever *you* worked for, too," and finished with, "And *who were they?*"

A coy look blanketed Whitney's face as she kept her game going, and came back with, "Let's hear more of *your* story first."

The younger man removed his iPad from the leather briefcase on the back of his chair. He proudly set it up while continuing to inquire about who he was sitting with by saying, "This would be a lot easier if I knew your name."

She returned with a smile and a shake of her head.

Once the waitress delivered Whitney's second martini, Jeffrey began his story.

"It started in the elevator at the Warner Center…actually, the same elevator where I met you. There was this attractive Italian woman. At least I *think* she was Italian--"

"But you're *sure* she was attractive?"

He blushed and replied, "Yes. Very," resulting in a twinkle in Whitney's eyes.

Less than 10 minutes later, the world-class scenery beyond the panoramic window meant nothing. Whitney's second Dickens martini was a sip or two from being gone, and her eyes were glued to the iPad…loving everything they had seen and what continued to play before them.

The screen turned white. The lower section of a black woman's face appeared. In the center of the screen her seductive lips were covered in bright gold lipstick. In the lower right corner the words *Fort Knox…by Divine* appear. The model whispered, "As long as I have lips…I'll have lipstick." In the screen's lower left corner, the words *Lips by Cheryl Harris* appeared just before it faded to black.

Whitney was awed as she listened to Jeffrey explain, "See what I mean about it being *universal?* It's a unique 'One World' concept."

"It's a *brilliant* concept, Jeffrey. I can see why that cosmetic woman liked it so much." Whitney consumed what was left of her martini, then asked, "And you came up with the whole thing?"

The excited Jeffrey nodded, then held up his index finger and used it to point at the screen. Whitney was happy to oblige.

The white screen showed the lower section of a female alien creature's face with long, thin lips covered in electric white lipstick. In the lower right corner the words *The Milky Way…by Divine* appear. The creature said with a sensual growl, "wuS vIghajtaHvIS…wuS rItlh naQ vIghajtaH!" In the screen's lower left corner, the words *Lips by K'ehleyr* appeared as it faded to black.

A proud Jeffrey turned off the iPad. He took a drink from the still half full glass of beer, then with a hopeful grin he turned to Whitney to hear what she had to say. He knew she had been captivated. What he didn't know was that it wasn't just by the presentation, but by his enthusiasm.

After gathering her thoughts, Whitney only needed to say, "Jeffrey…they're fantastic."

Though he was appreciative, he also knew it was for naught. After all, what could these two unemployed people do with a lipstick ad campaign?

"It's a shame you're not in a position to do something with them," he said appreciatively as he turned once again to the Manhattan skyline, preventing him from seeing Whitney's sly smile that came as the result of some plotting. Her look then changed to one of deep concern.

"Even if I *were* in some position," she offered, "Legally, seeing as you were employed by AOR, the concept belongs to them," then shrugged her shoulders and tossed out an, "Oh well."

"Not really," Jeffrey answered while staring at the lights atop the Empire State Building.

Whitney raised an eyebrow.

He returned his attention to her, took another sip of beer, then reached into his inside jacket pocket to pull out a folded one-page document and waved it at Whitney.

She slowly reached for it, unfolded and scanned the words as if not believing her eyes.

The waitress arrived to see if Whitney desired another Dickens, and if Jeffrey wanted a fresh beer to replace what was surely the room temperature one in front of him.

Whitney's index finger quickly rose to put the waitress on hold as the advertising maven's mind raced. She looked at Jeffrey and asked, "And you said that when you spoke to Gail Burrelle, she preferred your visual campaign over that *other* person's, right?"

"Right. Other than the slogan, she wasn't impressed with Quinn's visuals *at all.*"

The excitement within Whitney was too much. She blurted out, "*I thought so!*" loud enough for Jeffrey to hear, causing *him* to raise an eyebrow.

Whitney turned to the waiting waitress and ordered, "A bottle of DP. Nothing less than sixteen years old."

The server gave a rapid nod of the head and departed for the champagne vault. This, of course, left Jeffrey confused.

"What's going on? What's DP?"

Once she answered, "Dom Perignon," Whitney also knew it was time to say what needed to be said. She took a deep breath and started with, "Jeffrey, if I tell you something…if I *say* something to you…" *another* deep breath, and then, "Will you promise to stay calm, and not freak out?"

Even *more* confused, he could only reply with, "Not to *what?*"

She pointed toward the window and ordered him to, "Turn around and look at the skyline. *Please.* For *me.*"

Sighing and placating her, he did as instructed.

Whitney grabbed the dark sunglasses from inside her purse and put them on. Rising from her seat, she came up behind the unsuspecting Jeffrey and sensuously whispered into his ear, "Ah, grazie. Lei e' molto gentile'."

His jaw dropped and his eyes went as wide as they've ever gone before.

He turned to her. They were nose-to-nose as Whitney provided one of her most adorable smiles.

A bit too loud for the setting, Jeffrey yelled, "It's *you! You're* the Italian woman! But…your hair? Your *accent?*"

People from the surrounding tables looked at the couple, and just as quickly turned away.

"A wig and language classes. At that moment I was in '*Italian mode.*'"

But Whitney knew there was more that needed to be said to this bewildered man. This bewildered *young* man.

Turning serious, she began, "Jeffrey, I'm…I'm not just the Ital--"

Conversely, Jeffrey had a few things *he* wanted and needed to know first.

"Do you know Whitney Quinn?" he excitedly asked. "Did you work with her?"

"No, Jeffrey. That's not it," she replied as she took off and tossed the sunglasses onto the table and securely grabbed his arms. "I'm trying to tell you, *I'm* Whi--"

"I am *so happy* to find you!" Joy was on his face. "Please tell me. You *said* you'd tell me. What's your name?"

She pressed harder on his arms and slowly enunciated, "Jeffrey, I…am…Whitney Quinn."

All sound and movement in the establishment ceased for Jeffery. People at other tables. The servers. The music. Conversations. Dishes being placed on tables. There was nothing. He couldn't move.

After a few seconds Whitney began waving her hand in front of his face to elicit a reaction.

There was none.

That was when the champagne cork popped. Jeffrey returned to reality, resulting in him remembering where he was and the last words he had heard.

He waited for the waitress to fill their flutes and depart before asking in a surprisingly quiet volume, "*You?*"

Whitney responded with a simple wink.

It became harder for Jeffrey to keep calm as he let out, "*You? You're Whitney Quinn?*"

She smiled and nodded, causing his response to become louder.

"*You're* the person responsible for me losing my job?"

This time she nodded with a bigger smile.

People at the next table were eyeing Jeffrey suspiciously. One of them nervously raised a hand to signal for their check.

"Yes, Jeffrey, I am. And do you know that today is the luckiest day of your life?"

"How do you figure *that?*" he shot back with as the sarcasm dripped from his voice.

"Because…" she intentionally delayed, "…*I* negotiated my Dorsett and Mathers *contract.*"

Not having a clue as to what that could have meant, he ventured, "And *that* means?"

Easing up on his arms, Whitney recited as if reading from a contract in front of her, "The rights to any intellectual property, such as marketing concepts, slogans or artwork, presented to a potential client not yet signed to a D-and-M contract pertaining to said property upon termination or expiration of this contract will be retained in full by the employee…" She looked up, grinned and said, "…and *that*, my dear Jeffrey…is *me.*"

Still not getting her point, he tried again, only more frustrated, "And *that* means?"

"As far as Dorsett and Mathers is concerned, the slogan isn't *theirs.* And according to that piece of paper in your jacket, it doesn't belong to AOR either…which means As Long As I Have Lips is *ours*. And since Gail Burrelle liked what *each of us* presented, we'd be crazy *not* to make this work to our advantage…and as a team." Whitney extended her hand to shake and asked, "Right, partner?"

Still seated, Jeffrey backed away enough for Whitney to see he didn't see it the same way.

"*Each of us* presented?" he uncharacteristically barked. "You *stole* my idea!"

As the volume of their conversation rose, Whitney noticed *all* the tables around them were being deserted

"*Hey!* How did *I* know you were in the business?" she asked. "I heard something that worked for an account I wanted…and I used it. How the fuck could *anyone* think something like this would happen? Think of the odds!" She calmed a bit. But just a bit. "C'mon, Jeffrey, admit it. If you weren't an advertising rep, would we even be having this conversation?"

Jeffrey didn't know *what* to think. His upbringing and business ethics told him that this was *not* an acceptable way to do business.

He stood, slipped the earpads and iPad into his briefcase and said, "Please have your driver get my box out of the trunk. I'll take a cab home."

Whitney was stunned at his reaction.

The remaining patrons watched Jeffrey walk away as Whitney yelled, "Are you *crazy*, greenie? You know who I am, right? I'm offering you a partnership to do great things! I'm putting that '*big account*' you've been dreaming of right in your lap!"

He turned and yelled at the same volume, "What makes you think I want to have *anything* to do with *you?*"

They were going back and forth like high school kids.

"What are you going to do? Do you have *any idea* how fast word gets around in this business? By tomorrow every agency will--"

"Where are we?" Jeffrey interrupted. "New Jersey?"

She didn't know why he was asking, nor did she understand when he added, "I'll stay here and sell *ad space!*" Then he turned his back on Whitney and angrily departed, leaving her to sit alone and speechless over the fact that she was turned down by a greenie…and a man. A *younger* man.

She picked up her cell phone and texted Stuart to "Drive him home," then proceeded to consume another flute or two of DP.

About an hour later the white limo was parked in front of a six-floor apartment building on 98th Place in Rego Park, Queens.

As Stuart handed over the box, Jeffrey respectfully said, "Thank you, and tell your boss I said thank you, too," then the upset man walked toward the building's front door.

Stuart simply looked at the building's address and grinned.

CHAPTER 9
One Of A Rare Breed

Not one decibel of the 9AM Thursday-morning street noise at the corner of 5th Avenue and East 61st Street made it through the triple-pane windows of Whitney Quinn's 31st floor apartment in The Pierre.

Just like Whitney's office, the furnishings, artwork and the view west over Central Park were impressive. *Very* impressive. Simon & Garfunkel's "At The Zoo" played in the background as she sketched a pair of lips and the slogan on construction paper atop the dining room table.

That was when the doorbell unexpectedly rang.

Because the doorman didn't call to announce any visitors, Whitney assumed it was one of the neighbors, though normally they would call first. Using the remote, she lowered the music's volume, then opened the door.

Standing in the hallway and flanked by the same two Security Guards who removed Wayne McCoslin from his Warner Center office, was Dorsett & Mathers Human Resources Director, Grace Salzmann. Known by her trail of empty desks and the apropos nickname, "The Terminator," she played the part to the hilt and enjoyed every second of it. In her late-fifties and close to six feet, Frau Salzmann was just overweight enough so her business attire always seemed one size too small. But it was her attitude and reputation that made employees quake. No matter what the circumstances, if The Terminator was told your time was up, she and her Security

Gestapo made sure it happened as soon as possible, along with as much theatrics and drama as she could provide.

"Good morning, Miss Quinn. Grace Salzmann, HR Director for D-and-M."

Whitney laughed in the woman's face when she thought about James Dorsett sending his corporate version of Murder Incorporated.

"I know who you are, Grace," Whitney said, still laughing. "What's up?"

"*Miss Salzmann*," the Director sternly corrected, then extended a gloved hand holding an envelope. As Whitney slipped it from Salzmann's fingers, The Terminator recited, "As you are no longer an employee of Dorsett and Mathers, per page nine of your contract you have forty-eight hours to vacate your company-owned residence. Your severance check and the details of your package are in the envelope. Your corporate credit cards and restaurant accounts have been cancelled. If you believe there are any discrepancies, contact the Accounting Department. You know the number. Have a nice day." Then the HR Director and her guards did an almost perfect about-face and marched away before Whitney could react.

But she *couldn't* react. She was stunned.

Whitney understandably expected to be told to clean out her office, the walk-in closet, vanity and bathroom. She knew she would lose the company cards, along with Stuart and the white limo. But she never thought about the apartment where she had lived since she was fourteen.

Whitney stood frozen in the open doorway trying to grasp the enormity of what had happened…and to begin plotting what she was going to do.

It took a couple of rings of the landline for her to return to the moment. Shutting the door, Whitney went to the living room phone, looked at the Caller ID, dropped the envelope on the sofa and answered with, "Talk to me."

"Lunch. Smith and Wollensky's," came from Adam.

"Gotta stop somewhere first. Meet me at eleven-thirty."

"Where?" asked the dedicated subordinate.

At 11:25AM, Adam stepped from the cab on the corner of 59th Street and Lexington Avenue and walked to the entrance of Bloomingdale's. He knew his way around the Men's Department fairly well, but had to work a little to locate the Lingerie Department and to find Whitney rifling through racks of thongs. He found it difficult to approach his ex-boss in such surroundings, and even more, the twenty-seven-year old had to maintain a professional decorum around the attractive, affluent, older women *also* thumbing through thongs, brassieres, bustiers and lingerie.

Because of his good looks and well-dressed appearance, he noticed a few women checking him out, which distracted him and caused him to momentarily forget why he was there.

"There you are!" Whitney called out. Adam turned to see her hold a sheer red negligee against her body, which was already attired in a print shirt, a pair of jeans and heels, as she asked, "Whatcha think?"

He had no words, and felt it was best to keep it that way.

Following Whitney around the store, Adam swiped files on his phone and read while they walked, giving his report on everything she had asked him to look into. The assistant began with, "He's twenty-four. Grew up on a farm in Montana."

"Tell me something I *don't* know. Keep going," Whitney ordered without altering her stride.

"The agency was K-and-K."

Impressed, she asked, "Karsif and Katz? They got the John Deere account a couple of years ago, didn't they?"

"That was your boy's baby. He got an award for it."

"Wrong! He got *two!*" Whitney proudly threw in, then led Adam to the brassiere section where she picked up a few, held each to her breasts and modeled before a mirror. Adam did whatever he could to look at the phone screen.

"Where'd you get your information?" she inquired, as she chose a couple of bras to purchase, then walked toward the Dress Department.

"A fraternity brother works at K-and-K. He knew Holland pretty well. How's this? While he was at college, your boy had a full-time job at a nursing home, helped his widowed mom on their farm, and he *still* held a three-point-nine."

Whitney sternly pressed, "C'mon, Adam, I want *dirt*...not a list of his merit badges." She picked a blue designer dress off the two-thousand-dollar rack, sat Adam in a chair outside the dressing room, dumped the bras, the red negligee and her purse onto his lap and told him to, "Talk loud."

The ever-obedient Adam did as he was told.

"That's what I've been telling you...there *is no dirt.* This guy is *beyond* clean. He's *squeaky*-clean. He's Mister-Clean-with-hair. A real All-American boy. He could run for President and win *because* of how clean he is. But, well..." Adam tried to restrain himself, though it wasn't easy. "...this may be more than we need to know."

Whitney called out from the closed door, "Let *me* make that decision."

Adam sat for almost a full minute to think about how he was going to present the information to his former boss. As he was about to speak, Whitney walked out of the dressing room in the jaw-dropping sleeveless blue dress that fit as if it were custom made for her.

Adam wasn't just speechless, it caused him to forget what he was going to say. The words came out as, "*Damn*, girl!" Realizing who he was speaking to, he speedily recovered, apologized and got back to business as Whitney modeled before the tri-sided mirror. Adam kept his eyes on the notes in his phone.

"Anyway...Mr. Holland seems to think women, *City* women, are sex-crazed, man-hunting, money chasing connivers."

"How do we get these reputations?" Whitney joked with her reflection as Adam continued.

"My guy said Holland's looking to return home someday to find *'Miss Right.'*"

Whitney again spoke to her reflection, with, "Dream on, farm-boy."

"Oh," chuckled Adam, "It gets better."

Whitney turned to him and said, "Save it for lunch."

At the cashier counter, Whitney removed four Platinum and Black corporate credit cards from her wallet and handed them to Adam saying, "When you get back to the office, make sure you put them in Frau Salzmann's hands," then used her own Black Amex card to pay for the bras, lingerie and dress.

They left Bloomingdale's through the 3rd Avenue doorway and briskly walked the nine blocks to Manhattan's famed steakhouse, Smith & Wollensky...with Adam carrying Whitney's two Bloomies bags.

Once seated, each ordered a soda and that day's special, a medium Porterhouse with a side of sautéed spinach. As soon as the waiter walked away, Whitney got back to business.

"Okay, hit me."

Adam whipped out his phone and picked up where he left off, "According to my source, a bunch of guys went out one night back in Montana. Holland had a beer, *that's all. A beer!* Next thing, he's saying how he's waiting for 'Miss Right' to come along before he gives it up. Stuff like that."

Whitney seemed only mildly interested, and asked, "When was that? College?"

Adam slyly took a mouthful of soda as soon as they were placed on the table, and answered, "How about at the 'Going Away Party' the guys at K-and-K threw for him a week before he came to New York City?"

The words stunned Whitney.

"Are you saying he's a…" She couldn't bring herself to say the word.

With a smile as big as the steak he was waiting for, Adam replied, "Yep. One of a rare breed."

Whitney's mouth opened…but no words came out.

After a few seconds Adam snapped his fingers in front of her face. "Miss Quinn?" There was silence, so he tried again. "Miss Quinn? Are you okay?"

She shook her head after coming around, then responded, "Uh… yeah. I think so."

They didn't talk much once the steaks and sautéed spinach arrived. But Adam could hear the gears in Whitney's head turning… and turning.

As she signed the receipt, she said, "Get me an appointment with Gail Burrelle asap."

"You're coming back?" Adam asked with excitement and hope in his voice.

"No. Just make the appointment, and don't mention to her that I quit. Got that?"

"You know, with you gone," Adam said, shaking his head as he continued, "I wouldn't be surprised if I got *fired* by the end of the day."

Standing up and taking her Bloomies bags, Whitney chuckled, "And I wouldn't be surprised if you got *promoted* by the end of the day."

Adam returned with his own chuckle to say, "Yeah…right."

CHAPTER 10
"You're Gonna Need Me In Your Corner"

It was a little after two o'clock when Adam returned to the Time Warner Center, stopped at the HR Department to place the credit cards in The Terminator's hand and got back to his desk, though from the moment he left the steakhouse he was unsure of what his future would hold.

Once in his chair, Adam heard the door to Whitney's office open. His head turned to see James Dorsett in the doorway holding a FedEx envelope. The mid-fifties, nearly six foot tall, always-distinguished-in-appearance co-owner of Dorsett & Mathers didn't look happy, and it was evident in his voice as he bellowed, "I want everything she was working on put on my desk in thirty minutes."

Adam could only give one response. "Yes, Mr. Dorsett."

Walking toward the assistant's desk and standing in the exact spot as Whitney when they were confronted by Pablo Arenas, Dorsett queried with all the authority of *the big boss*, "I want to know what happened that made her quit."

Starting with, "Yes, sir," Adam recounted the conversation with Arenas, including mentioning the one-or-two-too-many drinks, and ended with, "She walked into her office right after he said you were her fa--"

Not wanting to be reminded of his error, Dorsett cut in with, "Yes, I know what I said," then picked up the receiver of Adam's desk phone and hit two buttons. Adam watched with interest to see where this was going. Once someone picked up on the other end, Dorsett said, "Arenas? James Dorsett here. Yeah, hola and buenas dias to you, too. Listen, I need to make a couple of personnel changes and I want it taken care of right away. Write this down." He looked at the seated assistant and asked, "What's your name?"

"Adam Bryant," he replied, certain to be fired.

Returning his attention to the phone, Dorsett said, "Adam Bryant," then spelled the first and last name. "He's the new Director of Personnel. You're fired." Dorsett handed the receiver to the stunned Adam and without missing a beat told him to, "Call Salzmann. Have this guy escorted out of the building in ten minutes or you're next," then turned and walked away, leaving Adam with the phone in his hand…and dazed.

At that same moment the B-52's "Love Shack" was loudly playing in Whitney's apartment. Sitting on the sofa eyeing sketch pads and poster boards of the lipstick ad artwork, Whitney was still plotting…to the point of coyly talking to herself.

"He's smart. He has manners and *waaaay* too much integrity for *this* business. And…a *virgin*. I haven't seen one of those in a *long* time." Picking up another poster from the sofa, she saw the envelope The Terminator handed her that morning. Tearing open its seal, Whitney pulled out paperwork detailing her corporate parachute and a severance check for $2.3 million. The amount didn't faze her, nor did she care to review the paperwork. She had other things on her mind.

It was Thursday evening around 5:30PM when the Uber driver dropped Whitney off outside the six-floor apartment building on 98th Place in Rego Park, Queens. Though only a few miles from 5th Avenue and The Pierre, the locations were worlds apart.

She was dressed as if it were just another day at the office, because in her mind she was about to make the most important presentation of her career. This was the one deal she wanted to close. It was the one deal she *had* to close.

Whitney approached the locked glass doors as a couple in their eighties were returning from an early evening stroll and walked up behind her. She scrolled through the call box looking for "Holland, Jeffrey." Having found it, she pressed the button and waited.

"Hello?" came from Jeffrey as the old gentleman reached into a pocket for his key to the building's front door. His wife was more interested in the woman wanting to enter and listened intently.

For the benefit of the eavesdropper, the executive seductively cooed into the call box, "Jeffrey, it's Whitney Quinn. I'd like to speak to you about the other night," then turned to the woman and winked.

His response was an immediate and definite, "*Go away!*" causing the little old lady's ears to perk up.

Whitney, knowing full well what she was doing, sexually sang to Jeffrey as she eyed the couple, "I think you'll like what I'm offering."

"*Go away!*" again came from the metallic speaker.

The woman leered at Whitney as they rushed into the building as fast as they could, quickly shutting the door behind them as Whitney persisted into the intercom.

"Look, let me in. If you don't like my proposal, you'll never hear from me again," then, like a teenager, she crossed her fingers and finished with, "I promise."

There was silence for several seconds…then the door buzzed, allowing her in.

Once inside, Whitney scanned the list of tenants on the wall to see he lived in apartment 3B. It only took a few seconds to catch up to the aged, slow moving couple waiting at the elevator. Once it opened, Whitney stepped aside, allowing them to board. The woman grabbed her husband's arm, indicating that Whitney should board first. Once she did, the woman held her partner's arm tighter as the elevator door closed, resulting in Whitney riding to the third floor alone.

She didn't mind.

The modest-but-tastefully appointed four-room apartment was a far cry from Whitney's place. Upon entering, the first thing she noticed prominently placed on an end-table was the framed 8x10 photograph of ten-year-old Jeffrey sitting on his mother's lap atop the tractor. Whitney admired the woman in her mid-thirties wearing overalls, work gloves and boots, with sweat on her brow and affectionately holding her son.

After being escorted to the sofa, the second thing she noticed was how comfortable she felt in Jeffrey's company...even if it *was* Queens.

Still unsure of why she was there and wanting to appear in control, inside Jeffrey knew he was out of his league. He sat in the chair across from her, each with a glass of Pepsi on the coffee-table between them, next to Jeffrey's iPad showing his lipstick commercials.

The screen turned white. The lower section of a woman's face appeared. In the center of the screen her seductive lips had sparkling green lipstick covering them. In the screen's lower right corner the words *Volga Green...by Divine* appeared.

Whitney smiled. Jeffrey smiled.

The model then cooed, "Poka u menya yest gubi...u menya budet pomada."

In the lower left corner of the screen the words *Lips by Polina Ivanova* faded in just before the screen went to black.

Once again, Whitney couldn't contain her excitement.

"Jeffrey, I'm telling you...this was destined. We both left our companies on the same day, practically at the same time. Then we met in the eleva--"

"I didn't *leave*. I was *fired*...because of *you*."

His words were heard, but she kept talking, "...then we met in the elevator...each legally able to make this whole thing happen. Here it is, right in our hands! And if we play it correctly, this campaign will blow Judian's away!" She seductively leaned toward Jeffrey. "There's only three things stopping us. The first is *you*. You've got to agree to be my partner. Fifty-fifty."

He laughed off her comment as if he was in control, though he knew he wasn't, and said, "What makes you think I need *you* to close the deal with Gail Burrelle?"

Whitney sat back and visibly restrained *her* laughter and sarcasm in any response.

"Trust me on this. You're gonna need me in your corner."

That was when his laughter and grin disappeared. "Trust *you?*" Then he cautiously asked, "What's number two?"

There was no hesitation in Whitney's reply.

"In order for this to work we've got to get in front of Burrelle as soon as possible...before my--" She reconsidered her words and closed with, "Before any *other* companies pitch her a campaign she might like."

A bit of sarcasm exposed itself as Jeffrey shot back with, "So...set it up. You got to her before I could last time. Do it again."

Just as fast, she returned fire with, "That's number three. Burrelle left town. My assistant can't find out where, and she's not answering my calls, texts or emails."

Jeffrey blurted out, "Are you saying there's something 'The Great Whiz Kid Of Advertising' *can't* do?"

Whitney gave him a hard look, but just as quickly realized...he was right.

With cool confidence he professed, "I know where she is."

The look on Whitney's face softened. She was impressed, so she urged him on.

"Where I come from, Miss Quinn, we *talk* to our clients. We get to know *them*...not just their products. That's just *one* of the differences between you and me."

"Uh, yeah…that's just *one* of 'em," Whitney comically and sexually thought to herself, then got back on track by asking, "And you feel you have a better knowledge of Gail Burrelle than I do?"

Jeffrey grinned and nodded his head.

Whitney reached across and gently patted his thigh. Leaving her hand there, she gave her patented seductive smile and assured him, "That's why this combination's going to work, Jeffrey. You're so much smarter than I am in the…*personal touch*. And from now on…call me Whitney."

He nervously looked at her hand. What little confidence and control he conveyed up to that point drained from him, and she saw it. She *very* slowly slid her hand away while dreamily thinking, "Yep…a virgin." Snapping back to reality, Whitney tried to keep things moving forward. "C'mon, get her on the phone. Just, uh… don't mention me. I think this will work better as a surprise."

"I can't reach her yet. She's at a retreat in Sedona. No phones or outside contact until Friday."

Without thinking, Whitney blurted, "Yeah, she does that, but usually in Italy," before catching herself in revealing more than she should.

Her words weren't caught by Jeffrey. He was too busy thinking of the offer Whitney had put before him.

Whitney, on the other hand, was thinking about the competition that wanted Gail Burrelle's account. She knew it was only a matter of time before James Dorsett would go after Divine.

Distressed, Whitney said, "We've got to get in front of her as soon as possible."

Jeffrey's confidence felt slightly resurrected as he told her, "She'll be at The Beverly Hills Hotel tomorrow for some fundraiser she's going to at night."

Whitney anxiously grabbed her phone and began tapping an app, "No problem. We can be in L.A. by late tomorrow morning."

Then without thinking, Whitney commanded, "Call the Beverly Hills Hotel Manager's desk. Tell Pepe you have an important message for Gail Burrelle, who'll be checking in tomorrow, and that he's to let her know you're flying in to have breakfast on Saturday morning. Leave your cell number in case he or Burrelle need to get back to you. Have him make eight o'clock reservations for two at her favorite table on the patio at The Polo Lounge. She likes it there and he'll do anything for her. Just, uh…don't mention me. I think this'll work better as a surprise."

"Okay," he quickly responded, then did a doubletake with, "How do you know that?"

Whitney gave a sly smile and quipped, "Trust me…you don't know *everything* about Gail Burrelle." Then she set about taking care of business as Jeffrey watched.

"How soon can you be packed?" she asked.

"An hour."

Again, she chuckled and said, "I'm gonna need a little more than that."

It was only two minutes later before Whitney confirmed their First-Class seats on an early morning flight from JFK to LAX. A few more moments and they were booked into a two-bedroom bungalow at The Beverly Hills Hotel. Then she called her longtime driver and arranged to be picked up at her apartment pre-sunrise on Friday morning, followed by collecting Jeffrey in Queens before getting to the airport. Even though she was no longer employed by D&M, Stuart happily assured her he would be there.

Watching her put the pieces together, Jeffrey became energized and ecstatic to be back in the game, and slightly enamored at Whitney's motivation and drive. He hit the remote for the iPad, causing it to begin playing all of the As Long As I Have Lips videos.

Putting her phone down, she reached her right hand out to Jeffrey, and with a sparkle in her eyes, asked, "Partners?"

Being the gentleman he was, Jeffrey stood, stepped toward her and shook her hand.

"Partners."

Jeffrey Googled the hotel's number and as soon as someone answered said, "Good afternoon. The Hotel Manager's Office, please." He was asked a question, to which he answered with authority, "Jeffrey Holland…of Holland and Quinn."

Whitney was smitten as she watched him and gave a little laugh at hearing their new company's name.

CHAPTER 11
"As For Me? I'm Going To Enjoy Myself"

Jeffrey was awed at Whitney's four large pieces of Louis Vuitton luggage that Stuart had taken from the white limo's sizable trunk at JFK, and just as awed when the driver at LAX loaded them into *another* stretch limo's trunk. Jeffrey, never letting his soft leather briefcase leave his side or shoulder, had only one suitcase…and there were no logos on it.

Just as New York City had been a new destination and experience to Jeffrey five months earlier, so now was The City Of Angels. The limo made its way from the airport along Century Blvd, then onto the ramp of late-Friday morning bumper-to-bumper 405 Freeway traffic heading north. Jeffrey laughed to himself as he thought of the ever-flowing movement of vehicles in his Montana community. The only time there was traffic in Pine Creek was during the Fourth of July parades when they had to close down Main Street for two hours.

Exiting at Sunset Blvd, Jeffrey unsuccessfully avoided looking like a tourist as his head spun from one window to another while the limo maneuvered past mansion after mansion along the palm tree-lined eastbound lanes of sightseers, commuters and normal daily traffic while the more-than-occasional Bentleys, Rolls Royces, Maseratis, Ferraris, Lamborghinis, Jaguars and Maybachs passed by. To Jeffrey, those were vehicles he had only seen in movies and on TV.

With each expression of the younger man's excitement, Whitney felt an enjoyable inner twinge of teenage attraction…and knew she needed to keep it inside.

Traffic thinned as they cruised into Beverly Hills before turning left on North Crescent Drive to navigate the famous hotel's driveway toward the historic canopied entrance. Three of the valet staff surrounded the car to open the rear passenger doors and remove the five pieces of luggage from the trunk.

Like most first-timers and tourists, Jeffrey, with his leather briefcase slung over one of his shoulders, was captivated upon stepping into the lobby. Following the fragrance, he leisurely strolled directly to the massive, elegantly flowered centerpiece. Whitney went to the front desk to check into their Crescent Bungalow Suite. He eventually walked over and watched as Whitney was handed her black Amex card and the receipt showing the room rate of $2,900 per night, plus a slew of taxes.

He did what he could to hide his shock and followed the two bellmen and two carts of luggage out onto the tropically floral pathways leading to the bungalows. Jeffrey then slowed his pace to put some distance between the bellmen and nervously asked Whitney, "Did we really need a bungalow at twenty-nine hundred dollars a night...for *three nights?*"

"We may need a fourth," Whitney answered offhandedly. "Don't bitch. It's usually thirty-six hundred a night, but I got a deal. If you prefer, I could get a one bedroom for two-grand. Is that something you want to do?"

Jeffrey's nervousness showed in the volume of his reply.

"No! It's *not!* And that's not the point! How are we going to pay for this? The airfares? The limos? Neither of us are on expense accounts anymore!"

Whitney's response was quick.

"If we do this right and sell Burrelle on As Long As I Have Lips, we'll cover this trip before the bills even hit. From this campaign alone we can open an office wherever we'd like." Whitney looked at Jeffrey. He appeared a little calmer as she kept going, "And if we *don't* get the account, don't worry about it. I'll take care of the expenses. Consider it a gift from Dorsett and Mathers."

Unsure of the D&M comment, he countered with, "I'm sorry, but I can't let you do that. Where I come from--"

She cut him off to say, "We're partners, Jeffrey. It's a business expense. And look around." Whitney pointed to the opulence surrounding them. "We're not *where you're from* anymore."

As they walked, the bellmen closed in on their bungalow, so Jeffrey tried again.

"What's wrong with the rooms in the hotel? I'm sure they're *quite* sufficient."

Whitney, remaining cool replied, "Burrelle will be staying in the Palm Bungalow, right? How would it look if we came here to sell your campaign and not show her that Quinn and Holland are up to her standards?"

He didn't respond. He was thinking of the company name she had just mentioned. Then, after a short pause, said, "Holland and Quinn. It sounds better. Think about it."

Whitney stopped walking and spoke the combinations to herself a few times, then nodded, "It *does*. Okay. Holland and Quinn."

His first real victory.

They continued toward the now opened bungalow door and stepped inside.

Jeffrey had never seen anything like the elegant two-bedroom suite with its spacious living room and dining room. Whitney began telling the bellmen where to place her luggage. Dealing with Jeffrey's was easier.

After he placed his briefcase on the dining room table, Jeffrey watched the bellmen step from each bedroom and stand before him. As Whitney watched, she saw Jeffrey go into his pocket and hand each bellman five dollars. Quickly opening her purse, and to Jeffrey's surprise, Whitney took two twenties from her wallet and handed one to each of them.

The men politely and professionally bowed, did an about-face and departed.

"Twenty-five dollars? *Each?*"

She smiled and silently returned to her bedroom, this time with Jeffrey not far behind asking a renewed line of questions, but he stopped dead as he watched Whitney unpack her luggage with almost military precision.

"I can't believe you brought all of this for only a few days. It looks like you emptied your apartment."

Whitney continued unpacking and hid a guilty expression as she repeated her mantra of, "How many times have I already told you, and will have to tell you in the future, 'We're going up against the *big boys* for the *big prize*, so we have to play on the same level, or go--'"

Jeffrey completed the phrase as he thought she would.

"Or go back to whatever little farm town I came from...and get plowed!" He cynically shook his head and finished with, "Very professional, *partner*."

Whitney stopped what she was doing, stood tall, took a deep breath and focused all of her attention and words toward him. "Get over it, Jeffrey. That was before I saw what you came up with and what you could do," she said with a chuckle in her voice, leaving Jeffrey unsure if he was just told off...or complimented. Whitney continued with, "As for me? I'm going to enjoy myself."

"And that means?" Jeffrey asked...almost afraid of the answer.

"Be ready for dinner by six. I want us in bed early," she commanded.

Jeffrey had no comeback. He was speechless. Fortunately, Whitney kept speaking.

"We've got to be ready for breakfast with Burrelle."

The only thing he could think of doing was to back out of her bedroom...which he did. Whitney followed as far as the doorway, then watched him walk to the living room's sofa and drop onto it, flushed and flustered. She smiled, closed the door and stepped back inside.

CHAPTER 12
"What The Hell Is Holland Doing In Europe?"

At the same time Jeffrey was unpacking his suitcase in the elegant bungalow, Rekha Vajpayee was standing before David Ruppert's desk. His two partners, Fred O'Connell and Vincent Arthur, sat in leather chairs on each side of Ruppert...facing their prey.

Knowing she was going to be interrogated, the assistant from Mumbai with a downtown attitude prepared herself.

O'Connell threw the first question.

"Where's Holland?"

Rekha swung and hit back in her most innocent and efficient voice with, "Europe, sir."

"Europe? What the hell is Holland doing in Europe?" came Arthur's angry retort.

Rekha again calmly and professionally answered, "To the best of my knowledge...it's *always* been there."

Ruppert rose from his seat, sternly looked at her and barked, "You know damn well what he means! Where is he?"

Such volume and anger of a superior would normally cause most to show fear...but not Rekha. Her response was just as calm as her previous ones, only now she stared at the three men just as they stared at her.

"How should *I* know?"

With Ruppert still standing in the attack position, O'Connell tried to start a dialogue.

"Whitney Quinn resigned from D-and-M on Wednesday, the same day Holland left here. It sounds like collusion and they may have been working together. We want to know--"

"*Working together?* With Whitney *Quinn?* Are you *serious?*" She was practically laughing in their faces. "*Plus*...Mr. Holland didn't '*leave here*,' Mr. O'Connell." Rekha looked directly at David Ruppert, pointed at him and said, "*He* fired him."

Ruppert had enough. He rounded his desk, stood in front of Rekha and demanded, "I want his files and everything in his computer that had to do with the Divine slogan and campaign he was working on. I want it *all*. Do you hear me, Miss...what's your name?"

Putting her shoulders back and showing she wasn't going to take his shit, she answered at a volume equal to his, "Rekha Vajpayee. My friends call me 'Raye.' *You*, Mr. Ruppert, can call me *Miss Vajpayee*." Then she alternated her view to the seated partners and said, "Mr. Holland never used a company computer. Everything he did was in his iPad." Focusing on Ruppert, she hit the final blow against him with, "And *you* signed that release giving him the rights."

Ruppert erupted in front of everyone, "Maybe you didn't understand me, *Miss Whatever-your-name-is!* I want everything he had on my desk in thirty minutes or you'll be gone, too! And your clock's already started ticking."

Without responding, Rekha turned and left the room to the sound of the men grumbling behind her.

Once outside Ruppert's door, the woman from Mumbai turned and saluted it with her middle fingers from both hands.

Eight floors above Rekha's interrogation by the partners of Arthur, O'Connell & Ruppert, James Dorsett, CEO of Dorsett & Mathers, stood in front of the sofa in Whitney's office watching his company's Art Director, Melody Beecham, present posters and video images of the side-views of several pairs of lips , and "the slogan" in various fonts going across them.

After several seconds of silence, he asked, "And this was the slogan she presented to Gail Burrelle?"

"Yes sir," came the Art Director's answer.

Dorsett picked up one of the posters, walked to Whitney's desk, raised the phone's receiver and tapped two digits. It rang once before someone answered and he ordered, "Tania, call Divine. Use my name. Get Gail Burrelle and call me back in Miss Quinn's office."

Before Tania could reply, he hung up, examined the poster and nodded. "'As long as I have lips…I'll have lipstick.' I like it." Then he gave a sinister look to the Art Director, again picked up the receiver and tapped another two buttons.

"Adam Bryant here," came through the handset.

"Hello, Adam, James Dorsett *here*."

"Good afternoon, Mr. Dorsett," Adam professionally responded. "What can I do for you?"

"Everything going well in the new position?"

"Yes, sir. Very well."

"Good. I have a question. The Divine account." Dorsett could hear a change in Adam's breathing. "Didn't I tell you I wanted everything Ms. Quinn was working on?" Hearing silence, Dorsett took control. "Apparently I need to make a couple of personnel changes…and I want them taken care of right away. Write this down."

Dorsett looked at the Art Director and asked, "What's your name?"

Near frozen with fear, she answered, "Melody Beecham."

Whitney wasn't kidding about enjoying herself.

It was a beautiful Friday, May 10th around 3PM. A few people were swimming and floating in The Beverly Hills Hotel's pool. Most were in a variety of bathing suits stretched out on towel-covered chaise lounge chairs, some in the sun, others under tents.

Jeffrey entered the pool area wearing Ray Ban sunglasses, a "Montana State" T-shirt, sneakers, a new bathing suit he had just purchased in one of the shops…and carrying his cell phone. The expression on his face made it easy for those watching to know he was a first-timer…not just to where he was, but to anything similar. He had never seen anything like it because every summer, from childhood until he moved to New York, he had worked on the farm with his mother and the few hands she'd hire. After settling into the Queens apartment, Jeffrey took the train to Brooklyn's Coney Island to view the Atlantic Ocean for the first time. That was all he was able to do as it was a gray mid-January afternoon, the water was frigid and most everything was closed for the season.

Looking for his business partner, he spotted Whitney's belongings atop a chaise. He walked to the empty chair next to it and sat. That was when a pool girl stepped in front of him holding an armful of large cream-colored towels. He looked up at her, unsure why she was there.

Raising the towels, she said, "For your chair, sir."

Embarrassed, Jeffrey stood up as she prepared the chaise and asked, "Would you like something to drink, sir?"

Whitney's commanding voice came from behind the pool girl, "Two Bloody Marys, and make mine a double."

Looking magnificent as she stepped from the pool in her wet bikini, Whitney stood in front of Jeffrey, took a towel off her chair and began drying herself in the sexiest way possible. Flustered, he tried not to watch…but couldn't stop himself.

"It's a little early for a drink, isn't it?" he asked.

Whitney handed the wet towel to the pool girl, winked and answered, "It's after twelve, right?"

The girl nodded and departed as Whitney took a pair of sunglasses from her bag and put them on, then lowered herself onto the chaise lounge and slowly stretched out…knowing full well that Jeffrey was watching.

"*Now* do you see why I asked if you packed a bathing suit?" she asked with a twinge of authority.

She could see his discomfort with the new surroundings and the uncertainty of his future, his slogan and his career, and knew it would be best to break that tension.

In a playful voice that also contained the self-confidence she hoped would rub off on him, Whitney jokingly said, "Jeffrey, am I going to have to teach you how to enjoy yourself too? Take that shirt off, have a swim, get a tan."

It was as if he had momentarily given up. He stripped off the T-shirt, sat on his towel covered chaise lounge, leaned back and closed his eyes. That was when Whitney chose to lower her sunglasses and look over the younger man's physique...and smiled.

Her observations went unnoticed by Jeffrey until a cell phone rang, causing his eyes to open. Whitney, knowing it was her phone, reached into her purse, looked at the Caller ID and started the conversation with, "Go."

It was 6:05PM in Manhattan. Adam was standing outside of the Time Warner Center holding a box of his possessions and was visibly depressed. Hearing her voice in his earpad, he started walking toward 8th Avenue.

His first words were, "I'm available for work...and he knows about Divine."

Whitney quickly sat up, *very* concerned, and answered with. "*Shit!* How?"

From what he had just heard, Jeffrey knew it was something he should be concerned about. He opened his eyes, turned to face her and watched.

"Beecham, the Art Director...I mean the new Director of Personnel."

Whitney shook her head at the news and queried, "Does he know where I am?"

"Unknown," was Adam's response.

Jeffrey asked, "What's wrong?"

Whitney didn't respond. She needed to find out as much as possible before knowing what to tell her partner.

As the box-carrying-Adam crossed West 58th Street, Whitney told him, "We're meeting with Burrelle for breakfast and I'll close the deal a half-hour later. He won't be able to get to her by then."

"Wrong. He knows she's in L.A.," was his reply.

"Who's your source?" Whitney was more than a little concerned and Jeffrey could see it.

"Tania. It gets worse," Adam told her.

Whitney was not happy, and Jeffrey was confused.

"What's *wrong?*" Jeffrey asked again, but with more intensity... though trying not to have others in the vicinity hear him.

And again, Whitney's attention was tuned solely to her phone, so she didn't respond. She wanted to hear why Adam felt it was "worse."

"Hit me," she commanded into the phone.

Jeffrey made a fist, pulled back his arm a bit for effect, then shook his head and lowered his hand.

Adam imparted the bad news, "He's flying out and will be there tonight."

"*Shit!*" came a bit too loud from Whitney.

Jeffrey, again stunned by her language, looked around to make sure no one heard her. He was surprised to see that even though some *did* hear what was being said, they didn't care. They were in their own Beverly Hills state-of-mind by either enjoying their drinks, the sun, the ambience or the verbal and text conversation they were having on *their* phones.

She continued with, "Does he know where she's staying?"

The street sounds of the City could be heard as he replied, "That's 'unknown-number-two.' Any chance you can get to Burrelle any sooner?"

"I don't think so. She checked in about an hour ago and texted Jeffrey that she's going to some fundraiser tonight to save palm trees, whatever that's about…and to change the breakfast meeting from eight to nine."

Jeffrey offhandedly chimed in with, "It's for Lethal Yellowing Disease."

With the phone still to her ear, Whitney's attention turned to her partner, so he kept talking to fill her in on what he knew.

"It's caused by a single-cell organism transferred from one tree to another by an insect that feeds on palm sap. The organism infects the tree…eventually killing it. If an effective insecticide isn't found, the affected species will be wiped off the face of the Earth."

Once again, Whitney was speechless, impressed and enamored by the innocent man *all* of her concentration was now on.

Though she heard Adam speaking, she didn't respond. Jeffrey saw the stunned look on her face as she stared at him. He waved his hand in front of her…to no reaction. He heard Adam through the phone loudly asking, "Ms. Quinn? Are you still there?"

Fortunately, that was when the pool girl arrived with the drinks.

Without moving her eyes from Jeffrey, Whitney reached for the second Bloody Mary, causing the server to quip, "How did she know which one was the double?"

"Intuition," answered Jeffrey as she handed him the remaining drink and departed.

Still gazing at Jeffrey, Whitney put her mouth to the straw, took a long swallow and revived with a refreshing, "*Aaahhh.*"

Returning her attention to the phone, she heard Adam's voice.

"Sounded like a Bloody Mary. Feel better now?" he asked.

Smiling as she gazed at Jeffrey, Whitney gave a satisfied, "Yeah."

Jeffrey was mesmerized by Whitney's behavior…especially as she picked up where she left off.

"Now be careful walking on Eighth Avenue and talking at the same time, Adam, 'cause I need you to find out what you can. But…I need you to keep this quiet, too."

Crossing the busy avenue to get to the other side, he asked, "Is there a job in it for me?"

With a smile, she answered with, "C'mon, Adam...what do you think?" then hung up.

The conversation revitalized Adam and caused him to walk a little taller.

Whitney returned the phone to her purse, and again, still wearing an enamored smile, took a long swallow of her Bloody Mary, then looked at Jeffrey and asked, "A lot of palm trees in Pine Creek, Montana?"

Worried about the phone call Whitney had just completed, Jeffrey sat up and answered, "I told you. I make it a point to *learn* about the people I do business with. When Burrelle told me about the fundraiser...I did some research. I thought it would help us tomorrow morning."

Whitney proudly replied, "Nice work, Jeffrey."

"Any chance you can tell me about that phone call you just had?"

He knew it wasn't going to be good news because Whitney took a healthy drink of her more than half empty Bloody Mary first. So he prepared himself.

That was when another cell phone rang. Whitney knew it wasn't hers.

Jeffrey looked at his Caller ID and quickly answered with, "Raye?"

It was 6:08PM in Manhattan. Rekha was standing outside of the Time Warner Center holding a box of her possessions and was visibly depressed. Hearing Jeffrey's voice in her earpad, she started walking toward 8th Avenue.

Her first words were, "Any leads on a new job?"

"Why? What happened?"

Rekha wasn't quiet about it as she crossed 58th Street. The louder she spoke, the more pronounced her Hindi accent became, in addition to her "City jargon."

"Let's just say Ruppert's partners are a little tweaked about him signing the rights away."

"What's that have to do with you?" Jeffrey asked with noticeable concern.

His sudden change of attitude caused Whitney to ask, "What's wrong?"

He responded by shrugging his shoulders.

That resulted in Whitney consuming the rest of her drink.

Rekha continued her story as she reached the corner of 57th Street.

"He flipped when I told him none of your files were in the office…" The light changed and she crossed to the other side of 8th Avenue as she finished with, "…so he fired me."

Whitney watched Jeffrey's demeanor change to guilt and sadness as he said, "Oh, Rekha, I am so sorry."

Whitney reached across and took his untouched Bloody Mary, then put the straw to her mouth and took a large swallow from the tall glass.

Once she lowered the drink, Whitney asked, "What is it?"

Jeffrey held up his index finger indicating she'd have to wait. Whitney shrugged, sat back and closed her eyes…holding his Bloody Mary in her hand.

Though Jeffrey was listening to Rekha, his eyes scanned Whitney's body.

"It wasn't your fault, Jeff. I know the real-deal. I know you came up with the slogan. I know you tried to talk to--" Rekha suddenly remembered something. "Hey, did you hear? Whitney Quinn quit D-and-M the same day you were fired."

Jeffrey did his best not to sound guilty, and answered, "Uh, yeah. I…uh, I know about that."

"I wonder where *she is* right now?" Rekha asked. "I bet *she* won't have a problem finding a new job."

Jeffrey's eyes were still on the person Rekha was talking about. His silence prompted the former assistant to ask, "Jeff?"

With her eyes closed, he watched as Whitney brought his drink toward her mouth and sensuously sucked on the straw. Jeffrey was amazed, yet embarrassed, hoping that no one was watching.

"Jeff? Mr. Holland? Hell-ooo! Mr. Holland?"

Rekha's voice brought him back to reality as he moved his eyes from Whitney and responded, "Uh, yeah. Right. She won't have any problem."

"So," continued Rekha, "What have you been up to? You working on something?"

Trying to catch up with the conversation, he stumbled, "Huh? What do you mean?"

He was finding it hard to not let his eyes return to Whitney.

Rambling and walking along the east side of 8th Avenue, Rekha kept the conversation going.

"Work. A project. Are you bringing the campaign to another agency or cosmetic company? If you do, would you see if there's a job for me…please?"

Turning away from Whitney, Jeffrey smiled and answered with, "C'mon, Rekha…what do you think?" then hung up.

The conversation caused Rekha to walk a little taller.

6:09PM along 8th Avenue on *any* Friday is a busy place.

Adam, on a phone call and carrying his box, hurried out of a deli doorway without looking where he was going.

"C'mon Tania, I just want to know if Dorsett spoke to Burrelle directly, and what hotel he'll be staying--"

BAM!

Adam slammed right into Rekha as she walked amongst the throng of pedestrians on their way home from work.

Their cell phones, earpads, the boxes and their contents flew into the air, then crashed and scattered onto the sidewalk.

Whitney, her eyes still closed and Jeffrey's Bloody Mary resting on her belly, remained stretched out on the chaise lounge enjoying Southern California's sunshine.

Jeffrey admired her beauty as he laid back. Suddenly, his eyes looked down the length of his body. He visibly became embarrassed and nervous by what he saw. The bulge of his erection in the new bathing suit was obvious...and he didn't know what to do.

"Okay, what's that about?" came from Whitney.

Sure that she was asking about his erection, he gave an, "Uh-oh *Busted!*" look. Quickly grabbing a towel, he laid it on his lap and did a terrible job of trying to look innocent...just as Whitney opened her eyes, brought the straw to her lips, then sucked and sipped.

Jeffrey used the opportunity to roll over, erection-side down, and tried to hide his grimace of discomfort.

Whitney turned toward him and asked, "Who's Rekha, and what are you sorry about?" She chuckled, "Jeffrey, did you break some poor farm-girl's heart back in Pine Creek?"

Whitney had an inclination as to why Jeffrey was face down... and she was right.

Twenty-four-year old Jeffrey looked everywhere but into her eyes. His embarrassment was overwhelming, yet Whitney enjoyed watching him so much that she heightened the matter by *again* bringing the straw to her mouth and sucking on it.

He did his best to answer her question, "No! Not at all. Don't be silly. Rekha was my assistant, and a darn good one. Ruppert fired her...because of me. Because of the slogan."

Whitney laughed at his use of "darn," and said, "That's wild. *My assistant* Adam got canned today, too. Not to worry. Once Burrelle signs the contract we'll need 'em both." She took a second to consider something, then continued with, "It may not be a bad idea to have them get together," then she emptied the Bloody Mary.

Rekha and Adam looked at the contents of their boxes strewn across the pavement as people walked over and around them.

"You idiot! Look at this! Look what you did!" came from the pissed off female assistant.

Adam realized his error and tried to apologize.

"I'm sorry. Are you all right?"

Rekha wasn't done yelling yet.

"Look at my stuff! Look at these fucking morons walking all over it! Where's my phone?"

Adam painfully reached under his butt, grabbed something and held up a cell phone. Rekha stood, furiously took it from him and began gathering and placing her things in the box.

Still on the sidewalk, Adam again reached down and produced *his* phone. He then felt the side of his head for the now-missing earpad. Seeing it on the sidewalk, he picked it up, blew on it and put it back in his ear.

"Tania?" he asked, hoping she was still on the line.

"No...it's Rekha," came from the angry woman he had knocked over. He waved a finger to show he was still on the call as people continued to walk past them.

"Yeah, I think I'm okay," he answered the voice on the phone, though he was still looking at the angry-yet-attractive East Indian woman standing before him. "Listen, I gotta go. Just find out what you can, and remember, keep it quiet. I'll call you later." He listened to something being said and replied with, "C'mon, Tania...what do *you* think?" Then he hung up the call...smiling.

"What the fuck are *you* smiling at, hotshot? Good thing I didn't break any bones."

Temporarily losing his 'corporate persona,' Adam stood up and turned on his 'street attitude.'

"Yo, baby girl...I said I was sorry. Gimme a break. I just got fired, and I'm trying to--"

"You too?" she asked inquisitively, then got a little cocky. "And don't call me '*baby girl*,' homey. You're too well-dressed for that shit."

"Homey? Where you been? No one uses that anymore," then recalled what she had asked. "Me too, what?"

"You said you just got fired."

"Yeah," he said as he began to collect his belongings on the sidewalk and noticed the contents of her box. "You too?"

Their common bond of termination caused them to lighten up on each other…a little. Adam continued to drop items in his box as Rekha took inventory and looked around for anything they may have missed.

"Where's my earpad?" she asked just as they saw a woman unknowingly step on it as she hurried by…crushing it.

They simultaneously said, "Well, fuck *that*," then shook their heads, sighed…and laughed.

"Look," Rekha said with her normal mix of arrogance and sense of humor, "It's been a shitty day, and you slamming into me didn't make it any better. The least you can do is buy the first two rounds."

As the pedestrian traffic passed by, the two smiled at each other and shook hands during their introductions.

"Adam Bryant…unemployed."

"Rekha Vajpayee. So I guess we can rule out champagne, huh?"

He nodded as they raised their boxes and walked along 8th Avenue.

CHAPTER 13
"When Whitney Quinn Wants Something…She Gets It."

The dining room of The Polo Lounge isn't only elegant, it's historic and has been "the place to see…and be seen" for over a century.

Once Whitney and Jeffrey, each smartly dressed, were seated in a booth, Jeremy the Captain Waiter approached, presented menus and greeted them, adding, "Nice to see you again, Miss Quinn."

"Thank you, Jeremy. It's nice to see you again, too. It's been a while. We're on a bit of a schedule, so we'd like to order as soon as possible."

Once their order was in, and upon finding out it was Jeffrey's first time as a guest, Jeremy briefly relayed tales of those who graced the famous hotel's rooms, bungalows, shops and eateries since it opened in 1912. The old stories of Douglas Fairbanks, Mary Pickford, Howard Hughes, Marilyn Monroe, Clark Gable, Humphrey Bogart, Charlie Chaplin, Frank Sinatra, Marlene Dietrich and Rudolph Valentino were secondary to Jeffrey once the names Martha Raye, Myrna Loy and Gary Cooper were mentioned, as they each hailed from Montana.

That night's pianist performed the requisite soft background music on the baby grand. At the moment it was a mellow version of "Try A Little Tenderness." People were enjoying dinner as Jeremy poured sparkling water into the couple's glasses, and then walked away.

"Water?" Jeffrey asked his dining partner. "Are you feeling all right?"

After a little laugh, Whitney said, "We have work to do."

"True…but in the morning, about fifteen hours from now," he responded.

She looked him square in the eyes and said, "We don't have until the morning, Jeffrey." The comfort and relaxation he had amassed during their time at the pool departed in an instant as Whitney continued. "While you were in the shower, I made a couple of calls and got the address of that fundraiser Burrelle's going to." She raised her water glass and drank, then said, "No martinis until after we see her."

Confused, Jeffrey questioned Whitney with, "Why the rush? Why can't we meet for breakfast like she expects?"

Whitney admitted to herself that it was time to give up more information to her partner.

"Jeffrey…James Dorsett is on his way to L.A. to meet with Burrelle."

Stunned, he asked, "James Dorsett? The 'D' in D-and-M?"

She nodded and informed him that Dorsett wanted the Divine account and he was going to use 'the slogan.' *Their* slogan.

Hearing that, Jeffrey's voice grew louder than what would be considered normal for where they were.

"*How?* You said *you* owned the rights!"

Whitney's head turned left and right to see the reaction of others nearby. In a quiet tone she told him to, "Calm down and lower your voice." She took another drink of water and continued to open up to him. "Let's just say Dorsett has a personal interest in this. And I know him. I know how he thinks. He's very, *very* competitive…" She lowered her volume to a near-whisper and said, "…especially when it comes to me." Then she raised her voice a little and finished with, "But as long as we get to Burrelle first, we should be all right."

Jeremy and a waiter arrived with plates of appetizers.

As if reminiscing, Whitney told Jeffrey, "Not to worry. Dorsett and Burrelle have been in this game a long time, and they haven't seen eye-to-eye in years. Let's enjoy dinner, and then…we have to get to work."

"Bon appetit," competently came from Jeremy, then he and the waiter walked away.

Whitney began eating. Jeffery, overwhelmed, sat there.

It was 9:18PM, Friday evening in Manhattan.

Placed on one side of the many comfortable leather booths in Gallaghers Steakhouse on West 52nd Street between 8th & 9th Avenues were the two boxes of corporate possessions. Adam and Rekha, both a little drunk, sat next to one another on the other side.

The remnants of their dinner plates were taken away and replaced with their third round of martinis. They were also in mid-conversation about the people they had in common.

"…and they're in *California? Right now? To* meet with *Burrelle? Together?*" Rekha asked as if not believing a word she was told. Once Adam finished nodding his head to each of her questions, she expressed with conviction, "I can't believe Mr. Holland would have *anything* to do with Whitney Quinn."

Adam responded with a knowing smirk and the words, "When Whitney Quinn wants something…she gets it."

Defensively, and not because of the martinis, Rekha shot back with, "But it's not her slogan! Plus, she had *nothing* to do with the visuals!"

Adam sipped his martini, then attempted to calm his dinner partner with, "C'mon, Raye…they were *both* looking to land the same account. You-and-I know that in advertising if you can't get the campaign in front of your client…it's worthless. And let's face it, if she wanted, Miss Quinn could sell deodorant and electric razors to Hasidics. So as long as Holland sticks with her…he *can't* lose."

Rekha considered what he had said, then picked up her martini and knocked back half of it. Adam couldn't take his eyes off the woman five years his senior. He was captivated.

"And you know," he said. "Maybe if I stick with *you*, I can't lose either." Then he leaned close to Rekha and finished with, "You know what I'm sayin', baby girl?"

Whether it was the martini, her sense of humor or that she was attracted to the black, distinguished twenty-seven-year old Adam, Rekha leaned closer to him and cooed in his ear, "Ooooh, poppy," just before they kissed.

CHAPTER 14
"Why Don't You And Your Checkbooks Come On In"

Several limos, Rolls Royces, Bentleys and some high-end Teslas, accompanied by the standard array of Mercedes, Cadillacs, Range Rovers, BMWs and other vehicles of status appropriate for such events, were parked on South Camden Drive with their occupants making their way to the entrance of one of the many mansions along the palm tree-lined Beverly Hills street.

It was just before 8PM when one more limo pulled up. The valet opened the rear passenger door. Out stepped a suited Jeffrey Holland who quickly turned and assisted his partner Whitney Quinn, wearing the beautiful sleeveless blue dress she had modeled for Adam in Bloomingdale's two days earlier.

Offering her his arm, they walked toward the mansion's elegant entrance as she commented, "You're such a gentleman, Jeffrey. Learn that on the farm?"

"No...from my dad."

"Good man. He taught you well. You're lucky to have him."

A sad expression overcame Jeffrey as he softly uttered, "He...uh, he died eight years ago, when I was sixteen."

Whitney immediately reacted by stopping their forward progress as if she had become paralyzed, then removed her arm and turned to him. She was sorry to have heard his words, and he saw it. She also felt an inner anger at herself and Adam for not knowing about this sooner.

Jeffrey opened up and said, "He joined the Army after high school. After his hitch around nineteen-eighty-seven, he became an officer in the Montana National Guard, married my mom and started the farm. I came along in ninety-five. Then in two-thousand-eleven he was sent to Afghanistan. We were told his squad didn't come back from a mission. That was it. Nothing more."

Jeffrey knew he had to lighten the mood if they were about to meet with Gail Burrelle and close the deal...the deal that would be "the one" to change everything. It was also the deal that caused the last five days to be the craziest he had ever experienced in his very inexperienced twenty-four years.

Jeffrey again offered her his arm. Whitney, speechless, took it and resumed their walk.

Just as they approached the door, he told her, "He's the one who taught me right-from-wrong, truth, honesty...integrity," then innocently snickered, "He *never* would have made it in advertising."

As the two laughed at the reality of his words, Whitney instinctively rang the bell before Jeffrey's finger could get to it, then turned to him, her eyes filled with sincerity, and tenderly said, "If your father could see you now, Jeffrey...he'd be very proud."

Jeffrey returned the look and said, "And *I* know that if your father saw *you* right now...he'd be very proud, too."

She held back what she knew, then nodded as if agreeing with his words and began to lean in toward him. A couple of inches before their lips could meet, they stared at each other...momentarily lost in the other's eyes.

That was when the door opened.

"Hello, Sugar! Fancy seeing you here!"

Whitney heard the voice behind her, but couldn't believe it. She spun around to see James Dorsett standing in the doorway. Her reaction was *not* what Jeffrey was expecting.

"What the fuck are--" She caught herself...but just a little too late. "What are *you* doing here?"

Standing a few inches above Jeffrey and Whitney, Dorsett, dressed and polished to the nines, looked down, and with a sarcastic chuckle in his voice answered, "Is that any way to say 'Hello'? And after I flew all this way for a family reunion."

Seeing Whitney's startled reaction, Jeffrey, as usual, was caught by surprise, so he asked, "What's he talking about? Do you know him?"

Dorsett's right hand shot out to Jeffrey, along with the question, "Jeffrey Holland, right?"

Jeffrey gave a dumbfounded nod of the head as the men shook hands.

"My name is James Dorsett, and I'm--"

"Don't. Please," Whitney firmly interrupted.

Dorsett released Jeffrey's hand, then turned to Whitney and with more than a hint of arrogance, asked, "You don't work for me anymore, *right?*" Before she could respond, he returned his attention to Jeffrey and proudly said, "I'm Whitney's father."

Again Jeffrey was caught by surprise, but this time he couldn't contain himself.

"Your father?" he loudly questioned his partner. "He's your *father?*"

Leaning against the doorjamb, Dorsett continued to add to Jeffrey's stress and shock.

"Son...it looks like you're in for a *world* of surprises. I bet you even planned to use that 'As Long As I Have Lips' campaign she came up with, didn't you?"

Jeffrey was now speechless, so Dorsett turned his attention to his daughter.

"By the way, Whit, my lawyers say I can beat your contract... anytime." Then, with a sardonic grin, Dorsett said to Jeffrey, "So, I recommend you take what's left of your junior executive career, get back in that limo and head for Montana…because that slogan and the Divine account are mine. You got that, greenie?"

From inside the foyer came the voice of a woman asking, "Who are you talking to like that, James?"

Once again Whitney heard a voice she recognized, but finding Dorsett already there put an unexpected kink in her plan. Whitney needed to do some quick thinking, so she stepped behind Jeffrey, not wanting to be seen until she could come up with something.

Gail Burrelle, looking great for her sixty-three years, approached from behind Dorsett, who was nearly a decade younger. Two things were apparent in their voices whenever they conversed…a familiarity with each other, and sarcasm.

Stepping into the doorway, Gail saw Jeffrey and flirtatiously smiled…then looked at Dorsett and asked, "Is *this* why you've been hovering around the door since you got here, James? What's the matter? Afraid of a little competition? A little *younger* competition?" Turning to Jeffrey, she said, "It's nice to see you again, Mr. Holland. Is everything all right? I didn't expect to see you until breakfast. You did get my message about making it at nine, right?"

Before the much-younger-man could react or respond, Dorsett, now with a devilish grin on his face, jumped in with, "That's nothing, Gail…wait until you see this."

Gently nudging Jeffrey to the side, Whitney was now visible.

Shocked, Gail boisterously asked, "*Whitney?* What the fuck are--" She caught herself…but just a little too late. "What are *you* doing here?" She followed her outburst with a scrutinizing glare to Dorsett and demanded, "James, what's going on?"

Dorsett shrugged his shoulders and gave his best and most innocent "I don't know" look. It angrily frustrated the woman who wanted answers.

Before Gail could rip into Dorsett, seeing an opportunity, Whitney stepped forward and said, "I'm here with--"

"Gail! We're ready to start," said the man who came from behind and placed his hands around her waist.

Tad Merrick was in his late forties, handsome, athletic and rich. Whitney and Dorsett noticed Tad affectionately take Gail's hand, then he looked at the three people conversing in his doorway and politely said, "Good evening." Turning to Gail, he asked, "Friends of yours?"

Flustered and confused, she answered, "I guess you can say that. But I'm not exactly sure *why* they're here."

Dorsett aggressively jumped in to say, "*I'm* here to donate to your cause."

Tad and Gail raised their eyebrows…impressed. The statement caused Tad to ask, "And you are?"

Gail began the rollcall with, "Tad Merrick…this is James Dorsett, Jeffrey Holland, and…" with a quizzical look on her face, completed the group with, "Whitney Quinn."

Whitney, her brain's gears turning and holding back any audible sarcasm, asked, "So tell us, Mr. Dorsett…what exactly *is* their cause you're donating to?"

Agitated at the spot Whitney had put him in, he quickly recalled the cover of a brochure seen on a table in the foyer when he arrived, and sputtered, "It's for, uh…for, it's something about…trees."

Unseen by the others, Whitney pushed a nervous and confused Jeffrey forward.

He got the hint and started, "It's…it's for Lethal Yellowing Disease. Commonly known as LYD."

Everyone's attention went to Jeffrey. He looked directly at Dorsett.

"It's caused by a single-cell organism. Once infected, the organism kills the tree. If an insecticide isn't found, the affected species will be eradicated from the face of the Earth."

Tad and Gail were duly impressed. Dorsett was pissed. Whitney was beaming.

"And *we'd* like to donate to make sure that never happens!" Whitney added.

Tad cheerfully told the three, "Then why don't you and your checkbooks come on in…we're just about to start," as he and Gail led Dorsett, Jeffrey and Whitney from the foyer into the living room.

Dorsett wasn't happy to see Gail with Tad.

Jeffrey was visibly dumbfounded, since the last two minutes had unexpectedly provided a massive amount of information for him to absorb.

Whitney was still beaming.

They headed toward the rear of the house as other attendees acknowledged Tad and Gail, and admired Whitney in her dress. Jeffrey walked next to her and angrily whispered, "Your *father?* What are we going to do *now*, genius?"

Strolling amongst the crowd, and as confidently as ever, his partner responded, "Easy, Jeffrey. I still have a few cards up my sleeve."

He looked at her sleeveless dress, rolled his eyes, then sarcastically-yet-nervously laughed, "Oh good. I feel better now."

It was a little past 9PM in the expansive backyard of Tad's home. The grounds were lined with lights, more palm trees and chairs. Those who came to speak about Lethal Yellowing Disease had just finished their PowerPoint presentation. That was the cue for the caterers to begin distributing hors d'oeuvres and drinks to the well-dressed, affluent guests as they began to mix and mingle.

Gail, Dorsett and Whitney, each with a glass of wine, and Jeffrey, with a glass of water, approached four empty chairs. As Dorsett and Jeff sat next to each other, Whitney and Gail stepped to the side and out of earshot of anyone else.

Whitney started with, "So…when did *you* take on palm trees as a cause?"

Gail's response was quick, and with her normal twinge of 'amorous' attached to it. "You *have* seen Tad, haven't you? Palm trees are one of his pet projects…" They looked across the yard to see Tad surrounded by a handful of women. "…and *I'm* another." Tad turned to see Gail and Whitney looking in his direction and sent them a kiss with a wave. Then Gail finished with, "He makes me feel *wonderful*."

"Can I assume *he's* the reason you want that extra hour before breakfast tomorrow?" Whitney cunningly asked.

"Fuck…you *do* know me pretty well, don't you?" Gail replied with a twinkle in her eye.

"Yes, I do. And you're bad. You know that, don't you?"

"Why? Because I like younger men?" Gail quickly replied. "All women enjoy them…when the opportunity presents itself. What about Holland? He's easily five or six years younger than you."

Whitney let out a laugh and said, "Holland? And me? No, he's a little too innocent, though he *is* adorable in a farm-boy kinda-way. Let's just say I'm not *his* type." She gave a sly wink and added, "And he's *nine* years younger."

They knowingly smiled at one another, then strolled arm-in arm back to the chairs, where Gail sat on one end next to Dorsett, and Whitney sat on the other, next to Jeffrey.

Having this unexpected group together and before her, Gail eyed them and began her interrogation.

"Okay…cut the crap. What are you all doing here?"

Just as each of them began to answer, Tad and a woman from *Save The Palm Trees of Beverly Hills* approached. She was holding an iPad Pro. Gail quickly regained her poise, but the tension between Dorsett, Jeff and Whitney was apparent.

Tad looked at Dorsett and got right to the point.

"So, James, now that you sat through our presentation, you mentioned something about donating to our cause...?"

Dorsett, flustered as he patted his breast pocket, replied, "I...I didn't bring my checkbook. I can have my office mail one in the--"

"Not a problem, old boy," Tad interrupted. "We take *all* the usual plastic."

Defeated in front of the others, Dorsett reached into his jacket, produced his billfold, took the Black Amex and handed it to the woman. She happily slid it into the chip reader.

Everyone observed Dorsett as the woman asked, "And how much would you like to donate?"

Dorsett looked at Gail, hoping to impress her, and said, "Five-thousand dollars."

The woman and Tad were very pleased and thanked him profusely.

The digits were put into the iPad and placed before Dorsett for his approval. He grudgingly tapped in his information and within seconds the woman returned his card.

"And Miss Quinn..." Tad began to say, but before he could continue, Whitney already had her Black Amex in her hand. She smiled, looked at Jeffrey, gave a wink and said, "Let's make it *ten*-thousand...from Whitney Quinn and Jeffrey Holland of Holland and Quinn."

Once again, Jeffrey went into 'speechless mode.' Tad was even *more* shocked. Gail's interest in the relationship between Whitney and Jeffrey immediately heightened.

Dorsett leaned close to his daughter and said, "That's a lot of money for someone without a job...or a place to live."

His comment pissed off Whitney, but that didn't stop her as she approved the amount on the iPad, tapped in her code and took her card, then said, "Maybe you didn't see the severance check Frau Salzmann brought with my papers."

He laughed and replied, "See it? You didn't look close enough. I'm the one who signed it."

Tad thanked them for their support and expressed how appreciative the *Save The Palm Trees of Beverly Hills* organization was to them.

"Why?" Dorsett asked. "With this crowd? You must get a *lot* of donations like that."

Tad laughed as he explained, "Not really. The average is around five-hundred dollars."

The eyes of Dorsett, Whitney and Jeffrey went wide…but their voices stayed silent.

"Not many people really care about what happens to palm trees," added Tad. "But you three? We must have made quite an impact."

The very happy woman and her iPad walked away to find more donors, but not before kissing Tad on the cheek. Gail stood and took his hand, again internally pissing off Dorsett, though he wouldn't let it show, and went to speak with other attendees.

Jeffrey angrily whispered to Whitney, "*Ten-thousand dollars?* You just gave away *ten-thousand dollars?* I'm out of work, you know that, right?"

Dorsett's attitude changed once he saw Jeffrey upset with Whitney. Yet to her it was all part of her plan…a plan she was still plotting.

While watching Gail and Tad meander through the party, calm and cool Whitney quietly answered the nervous Jeffrey with, "What are you talking about? You *do* have a job. You're the CEO of Holland and Quinn. Not to worry, partner. Everything's gonna be just fine."

Defeated, Jeffrey slumped back in his chair with his glass of water, looked at Dorsett still seated next to him and asked, "Is she *really* your daughter?"

Dorsett sat back, took a mouthful from his wine glass, slyly smiled and nodded his head.

About an hour later, Tad Merrick stood in front of his home's doorway waving to guests as they made their way to their respective rides.

Walking from the backyard into the living room were Dorsett, Whitney and Jeffrey being led by Gail, who told them, "I still have no idea why you're all here. But I'm sure it doesn't have anything to do with saving palm trees."

The three guiltily looked away.

Not getting a response, she kept going, "So I suggest we *all* meet at The Polo Lounge…at nine…for breakfast."

Whitney quickly reacted and responded, "No way! That's *our* meeting!"

Reaching the front door, Gail looked at the upset Whitney and, in her most professional of voices, said, "If you really believe you have a better campaign…don't be afraid to prove it."

With a touch of sarcasm, Dorsett looked at the still speechless Jeffrey and intoned, "Of course, if you think about what I said earlier, you may not want to show up at all." Then he turned to Gail and smugly confirmed, "Not to worry, I'll be there with *my* slogan and presentation."

Whitney confidently chimed in with, "We'll be there, too."

Jeffrey remained speechless, drained and ready to fly to Montana, which caused Dorsett to ask, "You don't look so good. Something wrong, son?"

Before the young man could respond, assuming he could respond at all, Tad approached and put his arm around Gail's shoulder. Dorsett noticed…and Whitney noticed Dorsett.

"Thanks again for your generous donations," Tad said as he tried to hustle the remaining guests out of his home.

The two donors politely nodded. Jeffrey stood there, distant and unsure of his life and career.

The father and daughter looked at Gail and simultaneously offered, "Can we give you a lift to your hotel?"

Gail gave her stock sly, sexy grin and answered, "That's very nice, but...no," then affectionately looked at Tad and continued with, "I'll see you all at breakfast."

Whitney winked at her, then took Jeffrey's arm and led him toward their limo. Dorsett looked away and headed toward his driver as the mansion's front door shut behind them.

"G'night, Sugar! See you in the morning!" Dorsett yelled to Whitney in the still night.

She smiled, kept her chin up and waved, but said nothing.

Their drivers opened the rear doors and everyone climbed into their respective limos, then the vehicles drove in opposite directions.

Once settled in, Whitney's first words were, "I want a martini."

Jeffrey weakly replied, "I've never had one...but I think it's time."

About an hour after *that*...

The lights in the bungalow were comfortably low. The opening notes of The Eagles "Hotel California" played through the living room's sound system. Jeffrey's iPad was on the coffee-table showing lipstick ads with the audio softly coming through its speakers...and next to David Ruppert's 1-page release-agreement.

The lower section of a woman's face appeared. In the center, her top lip was covered in white lipstick and her lower lip was in red. In the lower right corner the words *Polish Flag...by Divine* appeared.

In Polish, the model seductively said, "Tak dlugo jak mam usta...bede mjal szminke!" In the lower left corner, *Lips by Christine Wiśniewski* appeared as the screen faded to black.

Atop the dining room table sat an ice bucket holding a half-empty bottle of Ketel One vodka. Next to it were two extra martini glasses and a bottle of vermouth. All the makings one would need for a Dickens martini.

A slightly drunk Whitney, and a slightly-more drunk Jeff, were sitting on the sofa about two feet apart, wearing cushy Beverly Hills Hotel robes and each holding a martini glass. Whitney's, her third, was half empty. Jeffrey's, his second, was three-quarters full.

With an audible slur, Whitney asked, "So, Jeffrey...how are you feeling?"

Trying not to, but slurring more than Whitney, he answered, "Pretty weird. I've never felt like this before. It's..." he was careful not to mispronounce the longer word, "...interesting." Then he sat up, put his shoulders back and tried his best to sound sober and professional when he asked, "So, Miss Quinn...when did you decide you wanted to be partners...with me?"

She slid a little closer, leaned toward him, looked in his eyes and cooed, "When you left me sitting in the restaurant." He melted as she remained focused on his eyes and continued, "Later that night I was in bed masturba--" She caught herself and quickly changed it to, "*Meditating*...I was *meditating* and thinking of us doing *something* together." There was a Cheshire cat grin on her face.

Jeffrey wasn't sure what he heard, so he asked, "Excuse me? *What* did you say?"

Executing her ability of 'quick thinking,' even after two-and-a-half martinis, Whitney changed the subject, "So, feel better after your shower?"

Thanks to his already consumed 80-proof libation, Jeffrey's attention span was all over the place, causing him to look past Whitney to see the iPad and excitedly yell, "Oh wait! *Watch this!*"

At first his outburst startled her, before she realized what he was referring to.

She turned to see the lower section of a man's face on the screen. His lips were covered in black lipstick. In the lower right corner, the words *Black...by Divine* appeared as the model arrogantly said,

"As long as I have lips…I'll have lipstick…*bitch*." In the lower left corner, the words *Lips by 'Rocker' Monty VanderMay* appeared.

The screen faded to black.

Whitney laughed, shook her head, moved closer to Jeff and raised his martini to his lips while saying, "Jeffrey Holland…you are an advertising-fucki--" She again barely caught herself and kept going without missing a beat, "An advertising *genius*. Do you know that?"

He took a long swallow, nearly emptying the glass. Instinctively, Whitney reached and made little curls in his hair. He dreamily stared…lost in her eyes and accolades. Somewhere in his subconscious, something caused him to ask, "Want to…watch… another one, Miss…Quinn?"

Whitney put her glass down, reached and pressed the iPad's power button. It shut off.

"Not…right…now. And please…call me…Whitney," she amorously purred, then leaned toward Jeffrey, took his face in her hands, slowly brought her lips to his, closed her eyes and connected.

He didn't move. He closed his eyes and went with it, too.

The hand that was holding the martini began to shake, causing Whitney to open her eyes. Once she separated contact with his lips…his hand stopped shaking.

His eyes were still closed.

His lips were still pursed.

Whitney slipped the glass from his hand, put it on the coffee-table, returned her lips to his and closed her eyes.

His hand, still in the same position as if holding the glass, again started to shake. Without moving her lips, she opened her eyes, watched his vibrating extremity, smiled and began to place it on her thigh…now exposed from her robe.

Then, with a guilty look, Whitney reconsidered.

The beautiful, older, much-more-experienced woman put the innocent Jeffrey's hand around her shoulder and romantically moved tightly against his body as they continued to kiss…and as the intense guitar duet at the end of "Hotel California" slowly faded into Steve Miller's "Seasons."

CHAPTER 15
"He's A Gay?"

At 9:18AM on Saturday, May 11th, the street noise of East 32nd Street west of 3rd Avenue had no problem coming through the windows of Adam's fourth floor apartment.

Two boxes of office possessions were on the living room floor. A bottle of tequila, two empty shot glasses and a small bowl of used lemons sat on the coffee-table in front of the sofa.

Adam, wearing a robe, was in the master bathroom brushing his teeth.

Rekha, her hair disheveled, wearing a T-shirt and sitting in his bed under the covers, spoke toward a closed bathroom door.

"...and I *still* can't believe she left her job just because it got out that Dorsett was her dad. Big deal!" she exclaimed in disbelief.

The door opened, and with a toothbrush in his mouth, he said, "I guess she didn't want anyone saying her success was because her father owned the company. I've been with Miss Quinn for the last six years, and she really did achieve the things she did on her own. So, she had *her* reasons, just like your boss--" He reconsidered his words, "Just like your *ex*-boss...had *his*, you know, to live his life the way *he* chose." Then Adam turned and rinsed the toothpaste from his mouth.

"And that means...?" asked an unsure Rekha.

Adam came out of the bathroom, dropped his robe on the floor and slid under the blanket to put his naked body next to Rekha as he asked, "How long did you work for him?"

"I was with AOR for three years, and with Mr. Holland since his first day," she answered as she cuddled up against him.

"Five months ago," Adam interjected.

"How do you know *that?*" she asked, unsure how he knew such a specific detail.

Adam held her in his arms, smiled, but didn't respond.

Rekha remembered something he had said, so she asked, "What was that about living his life the way '*he chose*'?"

Adam was confused by her question, as he had the impression she knew all one needed to know about her former boss.

"You don't know?" he asked.

She could only shake her head.

With Rekha still in his arms, he probed, "Did he ever get any social calls from women?"

She thought nothing of the question and innocently answered, "No, not really. Just from his mother," then looked at Adam. He could only raise an eyebrow at her response.

After a couple of seconds of thought, Rekha's eyes shot open. She released herself from his hold, sat up and blurted out in her full Hindi accent, "*He's a gay?*"

Adam wasn't expecting *that* response and broke out laughing as he answered, "Not that we're aware of. But the boy still hasn't knocked-one-out-of-the-box, if you know what I mean. Well...at least not before he hooked-up with Miss Quinn."

Excited, inquisitive and now with her downtown attitude, she shot back with, "Stop it! How do you know?"

He opened his arms and she fell back into her last position as he told her, "That's not important right now. What *is* important is that I learn more about my little Miss Vaj..." He tried to get the pronunciation correct. "Vaj...pie. Yeah, that's it, right? Vajpie?"

Rekha found his effort cute, but had to correct him.

"Actually, Vajpie sounds naughty…but you're close, homeboy. It's Vaj…pie…*ee*."

Turning her so they were face-to-face, Adam romantically smiled and whispered, "Yeah, baby girl…that's what I said."

Their lips met and they stayed in bed the rest of the day.

CHAPTER 16
"I Thought You'd Be Halfway To Montana By Now"

The California sunlight came through the window of Whitney's bedroom where Jeffrey's face was buried in a pillow still asleep. Slowly he opened his eyes, raised his head and looked around. It didn't take long for him to realize he wasn't in *his* bedroom. He quickly lifted the blanket, looked underneath...and freaked out. He freaked even *more* when he saw his robe on the floor about four feet from the bed.

"*Where are my clothes!*" he yelled...then realized his head was throbbing. *Really* throbbing.

Already showered and in her robe, Whitney entered from the living room with a smile and sipping a cup of coffee.

Jeffrey was disoriented and hung over as he rubbed his head and eyes.

"Good morning, Sleeping Beauty. Or are you Prince Charming?" Whitney cheerfully chirped. She looked over his condition and asked, "How do you feel?"

He lifted the blanket again, saw his naked body and angrily asked, "What...happened?"

Acting innocent, she replied, "Coffee just got here. It's seven-forty-five. Get in the shower. I want to be sitting at the table when they arrive."

Jeffrey painfully sat up and reiterated, "I want to know what happened! Why am I in *your* bed?" He looked at the pillow and blanket next to him to see it had been slept in...realizing that he didn't spend the night in her bed alone. That shook him up even more.

"Later," she replied, "Right now, we have work to do. Let's go! Get your cute little ass up, have some coffee and then get into the shower."

She picked up his robe from the floor, laid it on the bed, blew him a kiss and returned to the living room, leaving him dazed and confused.

Two minutes later Jeffrey, wearing the robe, stomped out of the bedroom. As she drank from her freshly refilled cup of coffee and sat on the sofa, he angrily crossed his arms, stood before her and waited for her to say something.

She looked up and said in her most professional voice, "Big day ahead of us. Ready for it?"

"I want to know what happened last night! And what do you mean, 'Big day ahead of us'? After what your father said, do we really have a chance?"

Sitting back, she unemotionally replied, "Do me a favor...don't call him that. And remember last night when I told you, 'Not to worry, everything's gonna be just fine'?"

Jeffrey quickly shot back with, "*No!* That's just it...I *don't* remember last night!" Thanks to the hangover, the volume of his own voice hurt his head. He went to the dining room table and fretfully prepared a cup of coffee, then he cringed at seeing the vodka, vermouth and martini glasses still there.

Seeing Jeffrey's reaction, Whitney tried to calm him down somewhat by saying, "Tell you what, let's get through the meeting and *then* we'll talk about last night."

After downing a mouthful of coffee, Jeffery loudly wailed, "I was *drunk!* You got me *drunk!* You made me drink those martinis! And then we..." He became flustered and started rambling. "What would make you think I...with *you?* What would make you think I would *want to*...you know...with *you?*"

With a gentle chuckle, Whitney answered, "You didn't seem to be putting up much of a fight," then turned on her sexual charm and continued, "Actually, you were *wonderful*. And '*those martinis*'? You only had one...well, okay, two."

Hearing about the second martini, he nervously raised the cup to his lips and missed, causing coffee to run down his chin and onto the robe. Whitney couldn't help but giggle. Jeffrey was embarrassed, and angry at himself for allowing it to happen and being so clumsy.

He hurried into his bedroom and slammed the door as Whitney yelled, "Be ready to walk out the door by eight-forty!" Then teased, "And let me know if you need any help in there, or if you'd like me to dry you off!"

Whitney grinned, took a sip of coffee and sighed...enjoying her partner's innocence.

By 8:45AM the partners of Holland & Quinn, dressed for business and making a handsome pair, were being led to Gail Burrelle's favorite table by Jeremy.

As usual, Jeffrey had his soft leather briefcase slung over one of his shoulders.

Not yet apparent to The Polo Lounge's Captain Waiter was the tension between Whitney and Jeffrey, though the tension hit a highpoint when they approached the table for four...with the CEO of Dorsett & Mathers comfortably sitting at it, and once again, dressed to the nines.

Whitney did everything within her to appear calm and not react to his presence, knowing that the first person to show up for a meeting already held a position of power and control...starting with where they sat.

He knew it would piss her off, so he had gotten there by 8:30AM and was nearly finished with his first cup of coffee.

Dorsett stood and greeted his daughter with, "Good morning, Sugar!" Whitney all but ignored him as Jeremy pulled out the chair opposite the older gentleman. She sat without responding. Dorsett looked at Jeffrey, who was still dealing with the effects of his first hangover, and said, "G'morning, Holland. I thought you'd be halfway to Montana by now."

The clouded Jeffrey acknowledged Dorsett with a cordial bow of the head, then sat between father and daughter.

The adept Jeremy quickly read the room and its players, so he broke the ice with a smile and, "Coffee?"

Whitney and Dorsett responded in unison, "*Yes!*" then glanced at one another and briefly smiled at their familial similarity…then she diverted her eyes to Jeffrey.

Jeremy nodded and departed.

Everyone at the table was defensive.

Unexpectedly, Whitney almost-innocently said to Dorsett, "You're early. Afraid of missing something?"

"You need to remember who taught you to be fifteen minutes early for meetings where you want to walk away as 'the winner,' and know that when you meet with the person you taught, be fifteen minutes earlier than *that*."

Not backing down, Whitney played her first hand and said, "I don't know what *you're* going to show her, but if it's *our* slogan, you may want to leave now, because I wouldn't want to embarrass you."

Doing what he could to hold back laughter, he replied with, "Are you serious? Are you really thinking of going up against *me?* C'mon, Whit, I'm not some advertising schlub afraid to go head-to-head with you. You forget…I'm the one who taught you the game."

As Dorsett raised his coffee cup to drink, Whitney confidently retorted with, "And the mistakes."

Dorsett didn't expect her comeback, causing him to put down the cup without putting it to his lips.

That was when Jeremy arrived with Gail Burrelle...who was wearing a sexually satisfied morning-smile.

Once they saw her, Dorsett and Jeffrey quickly stood.

"Good morning, Miss Burrelle," came from Jeffrey.

"Yes, it *has* been, Mr. Holland. And good morning to *you*," she responded as Jeremy pulled out her chair.

As the three sat, Dorsett sarcastically tossed in, "Good morning, Gail. Sleep well?"

A waiter poured her coffee while she answered in a sexually satisfied tone, "Let's just say that when I *got* to sleep...I slept *very* well, thank you." Then she winked and grinned.

Dorsett burned inside at her response as he and Jeffrey watched Gail and Whitney lean toward each other, giggle and kiss the other on the cheek.

Jeffrey watched Gail whisper something in Whitney's ear, then Whitney whispered something to Gail. Both giggled again, then separated.

Jeremy distributed the menus and walked away as Gail got right down to business.

"Okay, Mr. Holland, what's going on? Four days ago you were working for AOR," then she turned to Whitney and said, "And five days ago you were at D-and-M. What happened to your job?"

Before Whitney could reply, Gail turned to Dorsett and sternly asked, "What happened to her job, James? And don't even *think* of kicking her out of the apartment!"

Dorsett, trying to be funny, said, "Oooops."

As Whitney sipped her coffee, she *also* tried to be funny with, "Too late."

Jeffrey shook his head as he attempted to put the pieces of their conversation together and exclaimed, "Well, that explains all the luggage." Then he stared at Whitney and asked, "But why would *she* care about where you live?"

Whitney and Gail simultaneously blurted out, "Later!"

Placing her cup down, Whitney replied to Gail, "I always said I'd leave if it got out that I was his daughter. You knew that. It got out. He took someone to lunch and said--"

Jeffrey interrupted with, "What do you mean, she '*knew that*'?"

Once again, but with more intensity, the two women barked, "*Later!*"

Gail disappointedly looked at Dorset and asked, "Three martinis, James?"

He made the face of a small child getting caught doing something wrong, and replied, "Four...I think."

"How many times have I told you? You can only handle two!"

Dorsett, though grinning, knowingly nodded. Jeffrey was confused by the familiarity of their conversation. Whitney was growing impatient and wanted the subject changed.

"Can we move it along here? Jeffrey...let's show these two what we've got."

Jeffrey removed the iPad Pro from his briefcase as Jeremy approached and took their food orders. Still sensing the friction, he departed as soon as he could.

Once the iPad Pro was set up to face Gail and Dorsett, the cosmetic executive asked D&M's CEO, "I imagine your company *also* wants my business...and to get it you'll present Whitney's slogan as your own. Sound familiar?" Before Dorsett could answer, she turned to Whitney and Jeffrey and continued, "And let me guess... that means you two have decided to join forces."

Whitney proudly nodded.

Jeffrey eventually joined her, but it took a few seconds longer. He was still trying to figure out the dynamics of the table's players. With the iPad ready to go, he asked Whitney, "Are you sure you want him to see this?"

His partner didn't reply. She gave him a proud smile…and a wink.

Gail once again turned on the sexual voice and charm as she looked at Jeffrey and repeated the words she cooed at their first meeting in The Plaza's Palm Court, "Okay…so show me what you've got…" She again sensuously pointed to the device facing her and ended the sentence with, "…in there."

The double-entendre went right over the innocent Jeffrey's head…again, but the others caught it. Whitney chuckled. She knew *why* Gail's words missed their mark.

Jeffrey tapped the remote…and the screen turned white. Whitney began the pitch.

"What is a One World campaign? Well, Miss Burrelle, let me show you the future…the future of Divine Cosmetics."

Dorsett leaned forward and watched with interest.

A few minutes later and after watching models repeat "As long as I have lips, I'll have lipstick" in English and several other languages, Whitney and Jeffrey were standing behind Gail and Dorsett. Jeremy, holding a pot of coffee, was perched between them. *All* were watching the iPad's screen, transfixed on the images and what they were hearing.

The lower section of a face appeared. A pair of lips with bright ivory lipstick were in the center. In the lower right corner, the words *Heaven…by Divine* appear. The model seductively said in Spanish, "Mientras tengo labios…tendre bile." In the lower left corner, the words *Lips by Silvia Fernandez* appeared. The screen faded to black.

Everyone appeared impressed, including the two who had seen the commercials countless times before. Even Dorsett was grinning.

Jeffrey tapped the remote and turned off the iPad. Jeremy filled the empty coffee cups as their food was distributed across the table and the two younger executives returned to their seats.

Out of nowhere, the Captain Waiter offered his opinion.

"You know, I'd look forward to seeing those commercials on TV just to guess which language the next one would be in. And I bet my daughter would love those colors, too"

The CEOs of Holland & Quinn looked at each other, then loudly and simultaneously said, "*Exactly!*"

Gail enjoyed watching their interaction.

Jeremy departed as the four began to eat their breakfast.

Jeffrey, with great pride, looked at Gail and kept the presentation going with, "The final scene with the lips and text, those would be your print ads. And we can expand the concept to fit *all* of Divine's products."

No one expected Dorsett to comment, but with more-than-a-little cockiness in his voice, he said, "I gotta tell you, Holland... that's a quality presentation you've got there. Maybe we can work something out. How about you sign on with D-and-M as a Senior Account Exec?"

Jeffrey smiled. He was being asked by a major New York City advertising firm to get back in the game. He was feeling good for the first time in a few days. Even his hangover had disappeared.

Dorsett then turned to his daughter and said, "And Whit, you can come back like nothing ever happened. You can even keep the apartment and rehire your assistant."

Jeffrey anxiously sat there...hoping Whitney would take the offer.

Gail watched...intrigued by the strategic game of Risk that was happening in front of her.

Whitney sat back as if considering the proposal put before her and her partner, then with confidence, she asked, "And if I say, 'No'?"

"You don't have much of a choice, Sugar," Dorsett said as he took two legal documents from his inside jacket pocket, then handed one to Whitney and held the other. "This is a copy of an injunction filed yesterday in New York. It says..." He looked at Jeffrey and read, "As an employee of D-and-M at the time she conceived and executed the concept, Miss Quinn, in effect, relinquished all rights to any intellectual property created while under the company's employ, causing all rights of said-property to remain with said-company. And that, Jeffrey, is me." Then he turned toward Whitney and continued. "Did you *really* think I'd agree to that clause without knowing if I could beat it? C'mon, Sugar...remember who you're up against."

Jeffrey was motionless. His life had just become meaningless... again.

"Face it...the slogan's *mine*," Dorsett said, driving home his point and their defeat. "Even if you fight it, the courts'll tie it up longer than your client will wait. There are a lot of agencies out there just dyin' for her to give 'em the word...and you know it. We *all* know it."

No one noticed Jeffrey body language. He was crushed and sure that all hope was lost.

Whitney didn't flinch. Though everyone was looking at her, no one could read her expression, nor did they have an idea of what she'd say next.

"That's not very fair, James," Gail interjected. "It's true. But not very fair."

Trying to appear as 'the good guy,' Dorsett imparted, "That's why my offer makes sense. Whitney and Holland get jobs, you get the slogan and we get your account..." He pointed to Whitney and Jeffrey, saying, "...that *you two* will handle and get one-hundred percent of the credit for." Then he pointed to the four of them with, "It's a win-win-win-win situation."

By this point, Jeffrey didn't know if he would walk away from the table with a job, a slogan, a client, a partner...or none of them.

Gail took control of the conversation with, "You didn't get my business thirty-three years ago, James. What makes you think you'll get it now?"

He responded directly to her with heartfelt emotion in his voice, "Because thirty-three years ago I was exactly what this kid is...a greenie. I had a great slogan, a great campaign, a great--"

"A great big ego!" Gail said with a laugh, then got back to business. "You lost the account to your boss because you couldn't keep your--"

This time it was Whitney who interrupted the revealing of Gail and Dorsett's history, with, "Okay! Do we *really* need to go there?"

Jeffrey continued to be intrigued by the banter between the three.

Whitney began to play the cards she said were up her sleeve. Looking at Dorsett with her best defeated expression, she asked, "I guess you'll want some kind of proof that AOR has no rights to Jeffrey's creative input in this, yes?"

Dorsett, knowing he was victorious, nodded.

Whitney took the one-page AOR release from David Ruppert out of her purse and handed it to her father. Gail leaned toward him to read it. Dorsett happily grinned as he neared the end, then returned it to Whitney.

"Well, that certainly clears Holland and eliminates AOR from the picture," Dorsett confirmed, then gave the smile of a winner to his daughter and said, "Glad to have you back, Whit." Then he turned to Jeffrey and said, "Holland...welcome aboard."

Once again, Jeffrey gave a sigh of relief. He had a job. Life was good...again.

Dorsett extended his hand, but before they could shake, Whitney shrewdly asked, "So you agree that this paper gives Jeffrey sole ownership of whatever he brought to the campaign, correct?"

Dorsett immediately sensed something was askew and retracted his hand.

Jeffrey sank...again.

Gail, slyly smiling, watched the interaction.

"Yes. Why?" Dorsett suspiciously inquired.

Whitney crossed her arms on the table, leaned toward her father and said, "Because I *stole* that slogan. I stole it and wrongly used it in *my* presentation."

Dorsett's and Jeffrey's eyes couldn't have opened any wider.

Gail was loving what was taking place.

"That means you'd be plagiarizing this man's work by using his slogan," Whitney went on to say, "It also means you have no rights to it in any way, shape or form. And since I was a D-and-M employee when I stole it…that makes *your company* liable for my actions, should Jeffrey file charges with the Advertising Board of Ethics and District Attorney."

The beautiful advertising executive sat back. She knew she was victorious.

Jeffrey *still* didn't know if he had a job, but was mesmerized and impressed by his partner's maneuver.

Gail, enthralled by the way things were going down, said, "Looks like she's got you there, James."

Like Jeffrey, Dorsett was now speechless, but quick to regain his composure. He finished what remained of his coffee, then again extended his hand to Jeffrey.

The youngest person at the table eyed Whitney, unsure if he should shake hands.

She reassuringly nodded and the men finally connected as Dorsett said, "You've got a great partner there, son. I'm sure you'll do some fine work together."

Jeffrey was still uncertain of what to say.

"Now let's finish breakfast and get out of here, I have to get back to my office. There are some personnel changes I need to make."

"On behalf of Holland and Quinn, we want to thank you for this opportunity, Miss Burrelle," Whitney said as she again reached into her purse for another one-page document and a Mont Blanc pen, then proudly said with a grin, "Let's make sure we take care of *all* the paperwork needed to make this complete."

Gail smiled and replied, "You're welcome and I'm honored to sign with the two of you." Then she turned to Dorsett and said with a twinkle in her eye, "And thank *you* for breakfast, James," and finished with a wink.

Realizing he not only lost the Divine account, Dorsett had to accept that he *also* just got stuck with the check.

Jeffrey eyed his partner with a new level of respect and admiration, while Dorsett raised his hand to Jeremy and made the universal sign for the bill.

CHAPTER 17
"Let Me Show You *My* Bungalow"

Under the blue sky of Southern California, Whitney, all smiles, leisurely walked arm-in-arm with her partner, still with the ever-present soft leather briefcase slung over a shoulder, along one of The Beverly Hills Hotel's pathways lined with tropical plants and foliage on the way to their bungalow.

In her hand was the signed one-page agreement between Divine Cosmetics and Holland & Quinn Advertising, or "H-and-Q" as they began calling it.

Several yards behind them walked Gail Burrelle, arm-in-arm with James Dorsett. Gail proudly admired the couple in front of them.

Dorsett saw the expression on her face and asked so only she could hear, "You're happy she got it, aren't you?"

Gail's smile widened. "I'm happy they *both* got it. Give them credit, James. They were both vying for my account and did what they had to do to get it. Just like *you did* thirty-three years ago."

As they continued to walk, and with Dorsett watching her, Gail took a tube of red lipstick from her purse, applied a fresh coat and asked, "Does it bother you to lose the same account twice?"

With honest resolve, he replied, "Maybe." Then with a combination of humor and sarcasm, he blurted, "At least I won't have to hear that old friggin' slogan of yours anymore." Sincerity gripped his voice as he then said, "You know what *does* bother me, Gail? Not being with *you* all of those years."

Gail wasn't expecting to hear those words, but it caused her to fondly look at the younger couple as she put the lipstick away and softly said, "In a way…you were."

Dorsett looked at her lips and asked, "Red Erotica?"

She gazed directly at him and winked.

He returned the wink, then pointed to his daughter and Jeffrey. "Do you think they…?" Not wanting to say the words, he finished with, "You think?"

Gail let out a soft laugh and answered, "Why not? He's smart. He's a gentleman. He's handsome. If *she* weren't with him, I'd be all over that."

Dorsett laughed and said, "Will you stop with the *younger men* already! Will you *never change?*" He again looked at the couple in front of them, referencing that Jeffrey was younger than his partner, and finished with, "Apparently, it's genetic."

Gail queried, "I thought you liked me that way."

Dorsett stopped walking, held her face in one of his hands and said, "No, Gail…I *loved you* that way."

He used his other hand to pull her toward him…and they kissed.

Unaware of what was happening behind them, Jeffrey slipped the contract into his jacket and let his mind drift.

Whitney observed him and wanted to know what was going on in his head.

"What's wrong, Jeffrey?"

Her voice brought him back to the moment.

"We just closed that 'big account' you wanted," she assured him. "Your ads will be seen all over the world. I don't get it. You should be pretty fucki--" She caught herself, but again, just a bit too late. "You should be pretty happy right about now."

"I *am* happy."

"No…there's something else going on in there."

Jeffrey became serious and the consummate professional.

"Whitney, if we're going to make this work, we should be thinking about the things we'll need to get up and running. An office, artists, equipment, staff, funding, we'll need to incorporate."

Offhandedly she replied, "Don't worry. I'll put Adam on it."

He just as quickly interjected, "And Rekha," then turned stern, or as stern as he could be, and said, "Plus...there's still last night to clear up."

Suddenly remembering his previous words, Whitney stopped walking, eyed her young partner and proclaimed, "Jeffrey...that was the first time you called me 'Whitney.'"

He raised an eyebrow and thought back several seconds, realizing she was right. It also diverted his mind off his last statement about the previous night.

They continued walking as he remembered something else that took place. Lowering his voice, he asked, "When Gail got to the table...what did you two whisper about?"

Looking down as if getting caught, Whitney quietly answered, "You saw that, huh?"

Concerned and still trying to control his volume, Jeffrey said, "And so did *your father*."

Whitney chuckled, "It was no problem that he *saw* us. He knew what we said. I just didn't want to make a big thing about it. And I told you, don't call him my 'father.'"

Once again, nervousness overcame him, and he was terrible at covering it up.

"A big thing about what? What did she say?" he nearly begged.

"She said, 'Good morning, sweetheart.'"

"And what did *you* say?" he fearfully asked.

Nearing their bungalow, Whitney softly and affectionately said, "'Good morning, Mom.'"

Shocked...*again*, Jeffrey ceased their forward movement and mouthed, "Mom?"

Whitney nodded, then tugged on his arm to keep him walking.

Once again near shock, Jeffrey watched Whitney swipe the bungalow's door key just as Gail and Dorsett caught up to them. Each looked a little disheveled…and Whitney noticed it.

Gail knew she was busted, but tried to make an excuse anyway.

In her best voice of innocence, she said, "Oh…I tripped into one of the bushes and James helped me. It got a little messy."

With a sly grin, Whitney whispered in her mother's direction, "Yeah…I'm sure it did."

Dorsett was distracted by the look on Jeffrey's still-stunned face. "You all right, son?"

Seeing that her partner didn't know what to say, and knowing it was best to change the subject, Whitney quick-wittedly answered with, "He's fine. I just told him about his commission from the deal."

Wanting to keep the party and family reunion going, Gail suggested, "Maybe a little champagne will help. Besides, I think we have something to celebrate…don't you, James?"

As they entered the bungalow's foyer, Dorsett answered, "What do *I* have to celebrate? I'm the one that lost…*again*."

As they led Jeffrey into the living room, he weakly uttered, "*Again?*"

Gail and Whitney simultaneously, loudly and humorously said, "*Later!*"

It took Room Service less than 15 minutes to deliver two bottles of Dom Perignon in ice buckets, extra ice and eight flutes, then arranged them on the dining table next to the vodka, vermouth and glasses.

Within seconds of the first bottle being popped, Whitney was distributing champagned-filled flutes to everyone.

The standard mix of soft rock music played from hidden speakers. Dorsett and Gail sat on chairs facing the coffee-table and sofa where Whitney and Jeff sat.

The now-coherent Jeffrey was in mid-conversation with Dorsett, who consumed half of the flute within seconds of it being handed to him as he reminisced.

"…there I was, fresh out of college, working at Carter and Brown. Divine was this new company with these crazy shades of lipstick. So I called Gail and told her I was a Senior Account Exec and had *the* ultimate campaign she was looking for."

Gail, with most of *her* flute already empty, interjected, "Pu-leeeeze, James!" She looked at Jeffrey and with a gleam in her eyes, said, "Three decades later, and he still thinks I fell for that story. Can you imagine that? The biggest agencies were lining up, and I let this green Exec-Wannabe talk me into dinner."

Jeff looked at Gail and Dorsett's visible age difference. Whitney, frustrated at having to hear this story *again*, went to the dining table, picked up the bottle of DP, dropped herself onto the sofa next to Jeff, refilled her glass and put her feet on the coffee-table.

"And it wasn't easy. She was all-business," Dorsett boasted.

Desperately wanting to change the subject, Whitney held up the bottle and asked, "How about a toast?"

Not wanting to stop the story Dorsett started telling, Gail continued with, "After dinner we took a walk along Madison Avenue. James was feeling no pain and acting a little playful."

Dorsett tossed in, "She introduced me to martinis. I was young. What did I know?"

Jeffrey sarcastically interjected, "Apparently it's genetic."

Whitney returned his jab with a grin as Gail kept the story going.

"In one memorable night James created a slogan, a campaign… and a dynasty," then ended her words with a romantic sigh.

Not understanding, Jeffrey asked, "What do you mean about the 'dynasty'?"

Now *really* wanting to change the subject, Whitney loudly interrupted with, "Can we have a toast...*please?*"

But Gail was on a roll.

"I had just put on a fresh coat of lipstick when James turned and kissed me."

"Red Erotica," Dorsett threw out. "I'm *still* a sucker for it."

Whitney swung back with, "*Apparently,*" then drank from her glass.

Loving the banter between father and daughter, Gail resumed the story.

"When he finally came up for air, he looked at me and in this sexy, romantic voice, said, 'Kissing you is like...kissing a fantasy.'" Gail followed her words with a reminiscent sigh.

Jeffrey realized that was the slogan Divine had been using since its inception, and was stunned to find out it was Dorsett who had come up with it...yet it was credited to Carter & Brown.

Whitney finished what was in her glass, then put the bottle to her mouth, turned it upside down, consumed what she could, and said, "And I thought I'd *never* have to hear this story again."

"Next thing I know," Gail rambled on, "We went back to his office where he put together the slogan and campaign that I've used ever since."

Whitney, proudly and slightly buzzed, said, "Until *now!*"

Jeffrey still didn't get his earlier question answered, so he tried again by innocently asking, "So where does the 'dynasty' come in?"

Gail leaned across the coffee-table and extended her hand with her empty flute. Whitney refilled it, then the cosmetic maven moved the story along.

"It was amazing to watch him work. Everything about him...I was just overwhelmed." She visibly and sensuously shivered as she drank a third of the flute. "Then...somewhere around midnight, we--"

"No, Mom...*please*."

"Why?" Jeffrey innocently asked, then turned to Gail to enquire, "We *what?*"

Knowing what was coming, Whitney refilled her parents' flutes, looked at Jeffrey's untouched glass and giggled at his innocence.

"In that little office, filled with all that creativity...we created something more valuable, more beautiful, more perfect than any slogan," Gail said as she lovingly looked at Whitney and tipped her drink toward her daughter.

Dorsett proudly nodded and smiled at Whitney.

Whitney raised the bottle and emptied its contents.

Jeffrey was amazed at what he had just heard, then queried, "You mean you...? *There?*"

Whitney walked to the dining table, removed the foil and wire from the second bottle of Dom Perignon and popped its cork it as she asked, "Will this torture be over soon?"

She realized it wouldn't...because Gail kept going.

"Two days later, James and his boss, Mike Brown, showed up to make the presentation. Of course, as most CEO's do for great ideas, Brown took the credit."

Dorsett and Whitney smirked, then simultaneously said, "Of course."

"*I* knew who really did the work. I knew who came up with it *all*," Gail continued, "But James was, well...*James*, and he got a little cocky in front of his boss. So they gave my account to one of their more 'seasoned' reps. It's been that way ever since."

Dorsett jumped in to say, "I eventually started D-and-M. But meanwhile, thanks to my slogan, Divine was growing."

Though Jeffrey's head was spinning from the multiple directions their stories were coming from, he thought to ask, "If you don't mind, when did you two divorce?"

Whitney refilled her flute, stood at the table and awaited the answer.

Dorsett and Gail fondly looked at one another, but didn't know what to say.

Whitney decided to let the two bask in the other's eyes and answered, "They were never married. They never even *lived* together."

"*Gosh!*" came from the innocent Jeffrey.

"*Gosh?*" came from each parent.

Whitney gave a loving look at her partner and told the others, "Yeah, he talks like that. Cute, isn't it?"

Jeffrey, still trying to get a handle on what he was just told, tried to cover up his naivete by saying, "I'm sorry. It's just that…well, where I come from…it's, uhm…it's a little hard for me to, you know…I mean, my mom would *never* do anything like that." Then he looked at Gail and asked, "On the first date? And you two were never married?"

Gail looked at her daughter and asked in her most innocent way possible, "Is he serious?" Then she turned to Jeffrey and told her side of the story, "Divine was just taking off. Was I supposed to give it all up just because I was pregnant or raising a child?"

Not knowing it was a rhetorical question, Jeffrey started to answer, "Well--"

Whitney tried again by holding up the bottle and strolling to the coffee-table to say, "About that toast?"

Dorsett decided to get some of his own narrative into the mix, "Actually, everything was fine…then she hit eighteen."

There was silence…which confused Jeffrey even more, so he looked at Whitney to fill in the blanks.

"Ever since I was nine I wanted to be in *advertising*, but I didn't want that 'child-of-privilege' stigma. So when I turned eighteen…I changed my last name."

"You never *did* deal very well with that, did you, James?" Gail asked.

It was apparent that with the consumption of champagne among the three, the conversation became more intimate and sarcastic.

James grunted, "I never liked that *song...or* that guy."

"What song? What guy?" Jeffrey asked, mystified.

Whitney kindheartedly answered, "Bob Dylan had a song, 'The Mighty Quinn,'" then pointed to her father and continued, "He always hated it...so I used it."

Innocently, Jeffrey said, "Sorry...never heard of it."

More than a little stunned, Dorsett and Gail looked at him. Even *they* didn't know what to say. So Whitney did.

"Montana...on a farm."

At the same time, the cosmetic and advertising executives emitted an, "*Aaahhhh.*"

Whitney continued *her* story, "Anyway, once I changed my name, *everything* changed. No one knew anything about 'Whitney Quinn.' I could be what I wanted to be and do what I wanted to do without anyone screaming 'Nepotism.'" Not wanting to take the conversation any further, she raised her glass and said, "So...let's toast!" Everyone raised their glass, even Jeffrey. "To '*As Long As I Have Lips...*"

Everyone chorused with, "...*I'll Have Lipstick!*"

Whitney, Gail and Dorsett emptied their flutes. Jeffrey sipped his.

Dorsett looked at his Rolex, put down his glass and stood to say, "Well, we should do this reunion-thing more often. But now, I've got to go."

More than a little obvious, Gail also stood and seemed to be in a hurry to leave, saying, "And now that I have my new slogan and a new agency, I should be going, too. I've got to call my staff. They need to cancel the pitch meetings lined up for next week." Then she looked at Dorsett and offered, "I'll, er...I'll walk you to the lobby, James."

Whitney and Jeffrey walked them to the door where Jeffrey shook hands with Gail and Dorsett.

As Whitney embraced Gail, she said, "Thanks, Mom." Then Whitney looked at Dorsett. It was a tender moment they hadn't shared in years. They each smiled. Whitney stepped into his arms and hugged. Gail, Jeff *and* Dorsett got a little teary-eyed.

"And thank you, too…Dad."

Once they separated and their eyes were wiped, Whitney, grinning, said, "And by the way, you were bluffing about that injunction and my contract."

"You know me too well, Sugar," Dorsett said with a wink. "I'm proud of you, Whitney. *Very* proud."

Then he kissed his daughter on the cheek, took Gail's hand and stepped out of the bungalow.

The couple held hands as they walked along the pathway. Dorsett began to turn toward the lobby as Gail took a tube of Red Erotica from her purse and applied a quick coat.

Just as they reached the door, Gail smiled and coyly whispered, "James, before you leave…let me show you *my* bungalow."

And show him…she did.

At the same time, Whitney was in full 'business mode' as she and Jeffrey walked from their bungalow's front door and returned to the living room.

"Did you see the way we meshed giving that presentation, Jeffrey? *Any* client would've bought that campaign…especially the way *we* sold it."

More excited than she was, he was ready to get to work.

"Then let's get back to New York," he suggested. "We have a *lot* of things to do."

Suddenly, overcome with being enamored, or it could have been Dusty Springfield's "I Only Want To Be With You" coming through the speakers, Whitney got very close to Jeffrey and seductively pouted her lips.

He pointed to her bedroom door.

She nodded, thinking that was where he wanted them to go.

He shook his head…confusing her.

"I want you to tell me what happened in there. And I want to know now!" he demanded.

That wasn't what Whitney was expecting.

They sat on the sofa as Whitney proceeded to tell him, "It started at the fundraiser. Then…we sat here and had a few martinis." She reached and curled his hair. "You were so cute…innocent…smart… adorable. I took you into my room, stripped you down, tucked you in, got in next to you, laid there for a while…" Smiling like an innocent child, she continued, "…then came back out here, ordered coffee for the morning, made another martini, watched some ancient Rock Hudson and Doris Day movie…and fell asleep," then patted her hand on the sofa.

Jeffrey lowered his head, torn between believing her or not. As he slowly raised it…he was smiling.

A big smile.

He pulled her close and spoke softly.

"Call Room Service and get another bottle of champagne in here…and maybe we *do* need to stay an extra day."

Their lips met.

After coming up for air, Jeffrey tightly held Whitney as he whispered, "Kissing you *is* like kissing a fantasy."

Behind his back, tears of happiness dripped from Whitney's eyes.

That was when Jeffrey lifted her in his muscular farm-raised-and-fed arms and carried her into his bedroom.

CHAPTER 18
Holland & Quinn Advertising

It was a very mild winter day in mid-February of 2020 in the affluent community of Alpine, New Jersey.

Yes, New Jersey.

A modern four-story office building stood on a tree-lined road called "Madison Avenue." Inside, the logo on the wall of Holland & Quinn Advertising greeted each visitor, along with the smiles of Tania and Nora.

Tania worked on her computer as Nora tapped a button on the phone console and happily said into her headset, "Good afternoon. Holland & Quinn." She listened to the caller, then cordially intoned, "Hold on, I'll connect you."

Whitney walked along the fourth-floor hallway. She was a very pregnant Whitney. As she waved while strolling by offices and employees on her way to her corner quarters, the diamond wedding ring on her hand was evident.

Entering Rekha's area, Whitney raised an eyebrow. Rekha knew her boss wanted to hear the most important messages instead of having to read them.

"AT&T called just to let you know their Marketing Department is looking forward to the new cell phone campaign...due, by the way, in three days."

"Shit!" Whitney angrily said to herself, which made Rekha comfortable working for a boss who curses. "I haven't even looked at it yet!"

Rekha lifted *her* very pregnant body from her chair, handed over the mail, and read from a legal pad as she followed Whitney.

"Lexus and Jaguar want meetings, like tomorrow. A VP from Judian Cosmetics would like you or Mr. Holland to call...and you have an appointment in one hour."

Making decisions as they walked, she ordered Rekha to, "Give the cars to Adam. Tell Judian we already handle a cosmetic company... and *what* appointment?"

Still with her downtown Manhattan attitude, the assistant said, "Uh-uh. See your partner about that one."

Stopping in front of Vice President Adam Bryant's office, he came out to greet the woman he owed his career to, and affectionately give his wife Rekha a kiss. Each of their chests were filled with success and pride.

Whitney breezed into the CEO office she shared with Jeffrey, who was sitting at his desk listening to a potential customer on the speakerphone.

A framed wedding photo of the two stood on a prominent shelf. Next to it was the photo of ten-year old Jeffrey and his mother atop their tractor.

Whitney dropped the mail onto her desk, walked to her husband, sat on his lap and listened to the call. The voice coming through the speaker was exuberant that he was, "...actually talking to Jeffrey Holland, and I hope you'll find the time to fit my company in during this year's slate."

Whitney wasn't making it easy as she kissed Jeffrey's neck and lips while he tried to conduct business.

The voice continued, "If you and Miss Quinn can do for my cars, trucks and batteries what you did for Divine Cosmetics...I'll never have to answer to the shareholders again! Just give me the word, Mr. Holland, and I'll send my jet for the two of you."

Jeffrey playfully struggled with his wife to disconnect their lips, then leaned toward the speakerphone and replied, "That's very nice of you, and please…call me Jeff."

Whitney continued to tease him and play with his hair.

"You have my cell number, right?" came through the speakerphone. "And you can call me--"

Whitney disconnected the call and continued to kiss her husband.

When she finally let him up for air, she asked, "What's this about an appointment?"

He grinned and said, "Your favorite."

A dozen pregnant women wearing sweatpants sat on floormats. An equal number of men and women of various ages and in various attire sat behind them. Proudly behind Whitney and Rekha were Jeffrey and Adam.

In the booth of a nearby restaurant, Adam was reading the small AT&T Instructional Manual to Jeffrey as the CEO held the new phone, pressing the appropriate buttons he was being told to hit. Their salads sat uneaten in front of them.

Whitney and Rekha were on the other side of the booth chatting away and devouring steaks.

All four were drinking water.

The men continued to discuss the phone when their wives' eyes went wide and grabbed their respective bellies. Each were hit with labor pains. The men were oblivious.

The women looked at one another, then signaled a waiter for the check.

It only took Stuart twenty minutes to comfortably get everyone to Hackensack in H&Q's new white stretch limo.

CHAPTER 19
"Sometimes You Need To Show
More Than You Can Write Or Say"

It was 1:47AM on Valentine's Day, Friday, February 14th, in the Maternity Ward of Hackensack Hospital.

Gail Burrelle and James Dorsett, wearing matching wedding rings, faced the window separating them from a roomful of babies. They looked at each other, smiling as much for themselves as for their new grandson.

Jeffrey joined them in looking at the newborn in a bassinet with the ID tag reading, "Jeffrey Quinn Holland."

A nurse rolled *another* bassinet into the room. Its tag read, "Raye Vajpayee Bryant."

Adam approached, patted Jeffrey on the back and the two "younger men" emotionally embraced.

Over the last nine months Adam had proven to be an asset to the company as a valued executive, and during that time, the two men had developed a close friendship.

Looking at his Rolex, a wedding gift from his in-laws, Jeffrey loudly blurted, "Shoot! I gotta tell my mom, but she won't be up this late."

That was when Jeffrey Holland realized the *next best slogan of his life* had just come to him.

He tapped on the glass to signal a nurse on the other side, pointed to his son and did his best mime to request that she hold him up.

As the nurse brought the baby toward the window, Jeffrey took the new cell phone from his jacket pocket, aimed it and pressed a few buttons.

In a semi-private room down the hall from where the fathers and grandparents were still admiring the newborns, Whitney rested in one bed…Rekha was in the other. Both were enjoying the quiet and solitude.

Sadly, it didn't last as long as they would have liked.

Adam and Jeffrey bolted into the room with Whitney's parents following a few seconds later.

Jeffrey sat on the bed next to a startled Whitney, looked at her confused face and said, "You may want to smile for this."

"For *what?*"

"I *got it!*" he boasted.

"You got *what?*" the new mother continued to pursue.

"Smile!" he ordered.

After being startled at nearly 2AM, and shortly after giving childbirth, all Whitney could yell out was, "Wait! I'm not wearing any make-up!"

"You look great." Then, with Rekha watching, Jeffrey cued Adam and said, "Hit it!"

Adam aimed the cell phone at his bosses, pressed a button and pointed as if to say, "Action!"

Jeffrey, with one arm over Whitney's shoulder, waved with the other and joyfully said, "Hi Mom! Meet your grandson. We love you, and we'll see you soon!"

Adam turned off the recorder and handed the phone to Jeffrey, who tapped more buttons.

"Will you please tell me what you're doing?" Whitney asked, trying to keep her temper.

He faced the phone's screen toward her. It showed a close-up video of her newborn son with the text below reading, '*Your grandson Jeffrey – Love Whitney & Jeff.*'

"It's our new AT&T slogan!" He faked an announcer's voice and articulated, "Sometimes you need to show *more* than you can write or say."

Then he hit the phone's Send button.

Whitney, ever the advertising executive...even after what she just went through, smiled and embraced her partner and husband.

But that was it. Jeff kicked into action.

"Adam! Tomorrow...meet me and the Art Department in the conference room by eight, so call someone now to make sure they're there by seven-thirty. And I want mock-ups by noon." Before Adam could respond, Jeffrey turned to the other new mother in the room and ordered, "Rekha, make sure we have coffee and pastry in the Conference Room, and...are you writing this down?"

Rekha sarcastically faked writing on an imaginary pad with an invisible pen.

Before Jeffrey could go on, Whitney took his face in her hands and pulled him close...so they were nose-to-nose.

"Excuse me," she lovingly said, "But...have I ever told you that you have a very beautiful smile..." She pointed to his mouth. "...and great lips?"

He stared at her for a few seconds and replied, "Ah, grazie. Lei e' molto gentile'."

Whitney put her head against her husband's, then they embraced and kissed.

EPILOGUE
...And Smiled A Satisfied Smile

It was around 7:15AM on Valentine's Day.

A rooster crowed from the coop on the side of a Pine Creek, Montana barn.

On the snow-covered main road, the brightly colored mailbox had the name "Holland" painted on it, which was a good third-of-a-mile from the farmhouse.

A brown and white Hereford wandered alongside the porch and nibbled on the twigs of dormant potted plants.

The walls and shelves of the master bedroom were dotted with pictures of Jeffrey through various ages, including many from his wedding, and young Jeffrey and his mom on their tractor.

Mrs. Holland, now fiftyish and striking, tied her robe's sash while walking to her desk against the far wall opposite her bed. Turning on the computer, she heard the familiar tone alerting her to new emails.

Resting into a comfortable chair, she guided the mouse and tapped a button. Within a second the video of the nurse holding a newborn to the camera filled the screen. The scene cut to a close-up of the baby with the text, '*Your grandson Jeffrey – Love Whitney & Jeff*', below him. The image cross-faded into her son and daughter-in-law on the hospital bed as he waved and said, "Hi Mom! Meet your grandson. We love you, and we'll see you soon!"

Mrs. Holland lovingly and proudly beamed at the images and sentiment on the screen...as a pair of strong hands appeared on her shoulders. They belonged to a man...a younger man in his thirties.

He was handsome and possessed a sturdy body…visible due to the open robe *he* was wearing.

A bolt of life and energy shot through the older woman as he romantically kissed her neck, then asked, "Will you be my valentine?"

She put her hand in his, led him back to the bed…and smiled a satisfied smile.

THE END

CAST OF CHARACTERS
In Order Of Appearance

Jeffrey Holland:	Twenty-four. From Montana. Ethical and innocent. Works for Arthur, O'Connell & Ruppert (aka AOR).
Rekha Vajpayee:	Thirty-two. Born and raised in Mumbai, India. Lives in Downtown Manhattan. Works at AOR as Jeffrey Holland's assistant.
Whitney Quinn:	Thirty-three. Advertising executive of the highest degree. The Vice President of Dorsett & Mathers (aka: D&M).
Vance:	A seafood company heir that was just a passing thing.
Stuart:	Whitney Quinn's longtime chauffeur.
Nora:	Receptionist for AOR.
Tania:	Receptionist for D&M.
Adam Bryant:	Twenty-seven. Black. Classy. Efficient. Works at D&M as Whitney Quinn's assistant. Then the Director of Personnel.
Paige:	Graphic artist for AOR.
Gail Burrelle:	Sixty-three. The owner of Divine Cosmetics.
James Dorsett:	Fifty-five. CEO of Dorsett & Mathers.

Wayne McCoslin: Mid-fifties but looks in his seventies Smokes cigarettes and never smiles. Director of Personnel for D&M. Has a nineteen-year old daughter.

David Ruppert: Mid-seventies. A partner of Arthur, O'Connell & Ruppert.

Melody Beecham: The Art Director at D&M, then the Director of Personnel.

Pablo Arenas: Custodian at D&M, then the Assistant Director of Personnel. Good friends with Wayne McCoslin's daughter.

Grace Salzmann: Late fifties. D&M's Human Resources Director. Known as "The Terminator." Just overweight enough so her business attire always seems one size too small.

Jeremy: The Captain Waiter at The Beverly Hills Hotel's Polo Lounge.

Fred O'Connell: Mid-seventies. A partner of Arthur, O'Connell & Ruppert.

Vincent Arthur: Mid-seventies. A partner of Arthur, O'Connell & Ruppert.

Tad Merrick: Late forties. Handsome. Athletic. Rich. Likes palm trees. Makes Gail Burrelle feel wonderful.

Jeffrey's Mother: Lives on a farm in Pine Creek, Montana.